All I Asking for Is My Body

MILTON MURAYAMA

Afterword by Franklin S. Odo

A Kolowalu Book
University of Hawaii Press

Originally published by Supa Press, 1975.
A slightly different version of ''I'll Crack Your Head Kotsun'' was
first published in *Arizona Quarterly,* and reprinted in *The Spell of Hawaii,*
edited by A. Grove Day and Carl Stroven.

University of Hawaii Press edition, published 1988
Manufactured in the United States of America

93 92 91 90 89   5 4 3 2

Library of Congress Cataloging-in-Publication Data
Murayama, Milton.
    All I asking for is my body / by Milton Murayama ; afterword by
Franklin S. Odo.
        p.   cm. — (A Kolowalu book)
    ISBN 0-8248-1172-0
    I. Title.
    PS3563.U723A79 1988
    813'.54—dc19   88-6967
                                                         CIP

FOR THE FAMILY

CONTENTS

PART I

I'll Crack Your Head *Kotsun*

There was something funny about Makot. He always played with guys younger than he and the big guys his own age always made fun of him. His family was the only Japanese family in Filipino Camp and his father didn't seem to do anything but ride around in his brand-new Ford Model T. But Makot always had money to spend and the young kids liked him.

During the summer in Pepelau, Hawaii, the whole town spends the whole day at the beach. We go there early in the morning, then walk home for lunch, often in our trunks, then go back for more spearing fish, surfing, or just plain swimming, depending on the tide, and stay there till sunset. At night there were the movies for those who had the money and the Buddhist Bon dances and dance practices. The only change in dress was that at night we wore Japanese zori and in the day bare feet. Nobody owned shoes in Pepelau.

In August Makot became our gang leader. We were all at the beach and it was on a Wednesday when there was a matinee, and Makot said, "Come on, I'll take you all to the movies," and Mit, Skats, and I became his gang in no time. Mit or Mitsunobu Kato and Skats or Nobuyuki Asakatsu and I were not exactly a gang. There were only three of us and we were all going to be in the fourth grade, so nobody was leader. But we were a kind of a poor gang. None of us were in the Boy Scouts or had bicycles, we played football with tennis balls, and during basketball season we hung around Baldwin Park till some gang showed up with a rubber ball or a real basketball.

After that day we followed Makot at the beach, and in spearing fish Skats and I followed him across the breakers. We didn't want to go at first, since no fourth-grader went across the breakers, but he teased us and called us yellow, so Skats and I followed. Mit didn't care if he was called yellow. Then at lunchtime, instead of all of us going home for lunch, Makot invited us all to his home in Filipino Camp. Nobody was home and he cooked us rice and canned corned beef and onions. The following day there was the new kind of Campbell soup in cans, which we got at home only when we were sick. So I began to look forward to lunchtime, when we'd go to Makot's home to eat. At home Father was a fisherman and so we ate fish and rice three times a day, and as my older brother Tosh who was a seventh-grader always said, "What! Fish and rice again! No wonder the Japanese get beriberi!" I was sick of fish and rice too.

Mother didn't seem too happy about my eating at Makot's. About the fourth day when I came home at sunset, she said in Japanese, "You must be famished, Kiyo-chan, shall I fix you something?"

"No, I had lunch at Makoto-san's home."

"Oh, again?"

Mother was sitting on a cushion on the floor, her legs hid under her, and she was bending over and sewing a kimono by hand. It was what she always did. I sat down cross-legged. "Uh huh. Makoto-san invited me. I ate a bellyful. Makoto-san is a very good cook. He fixed some corned beef and onions and it was delicious."

"Oh, are you playing with Makoto-san now? He's too old for you, isn't he? He's Toshio's age. What about Mitsunobu-san and Nobuyuki-san?"

"Oh, they still with me. We all play with Makoto-san. He invited all of us."

"Makoto-san's mother or father wasn't home?"

"No, they're usually not home."

"You know, Kiyo-chan, you shouldn't eat at Makoto-san's home too often."

"Why? But he invites us."

"But his parents didn't invite you. Do you understand, Kiyo-chan?"

"But why? Nobuyuki-san and Mitsunobu-san go."

"Kiyo-chan is a good boy so he'll obey what his mother says, won't he?"

"But why, Mother! I eat at Nobuyuki's and Mitsunobu's homes when their parents aren't home. And I always thank their parents when I see them. I haven't thanked Makoto's parents yet, but I will when I see them."

"But don't you see, Kiyoshi, you will bring shame to your father and me if you go there to eat. People will say, 'Ah, look at the Oyama's number two boy. He's a *hoitobo!* He's a *chorimbo!* That's because his parents are *hoitobo* and *chorimbo!*' "

Hoitobo means beggar in Japanese and *chorimbo* is something like a bum, but they're ten times worse than beggar and bum because you always make your face real ugly when you say them and they sound horrible!

"But Makoto invites us, Mother! Once Mitsunobu didn't want to go and Makoto dragged him. We can always have Makoto-san over to our home and repay him the way we do Mitsunobu-san and Nobuyuki-san."

"But can't you see, Kiyo-chan, people will laugh at you. 'Look at that Kiyoshi Oyama,' they'll say, 'he always eats at the Sasakis'. It's because his parents are poor and he doesn't have enough to eat at home.' You understand, don't you, Kiyo-chan? You're a good filial boy so you'll obey what your parents say, won't you? Your father and I would cry if we had two unfilial sons like Toshio . . ."

"But what about Nobuyuki and Mitsunobu? Won't people talk about them and their parents like that too?"

"But Kiyoshi, you're not a monkey. You don't have to copy others. Whatever Nobuyuki and Mitsunobu do is up to them. Besides, we're poor and poor families have to be more careful."

"But Mitsunobu's home is poor too! They have lots of children and he's always charging things at the stores and his home looks poor like ours!"

"Nemmind! You'll catch a sickness if you go there too often," she made a real ugly face.

"What kind of sickness? Won't Mitsunobu-san and Nobuyuki-san catch it too?"

She dropped her sewing on her lap and looked straight at me. "Kiyoshi, you will obey your parents, won't you?"

I stood up and hitched up my pants. I didn't say yes or no. I just grunted like Father and walked out.

But the next time I went to eat at Makot's I felt guilty and the corned beef and onions didn't taste so good. And when I came home that night the first thing Mother asked was, "Oh, did you have lunch, Kiyo-chan?" Then, "At Makoto-san's home?" and her face looked as if she was going to cry.

But I figured that that was the end of that so I was surprised when Father turned to me at the supper table and said, "Kiyoshi . . ." Whenever he called me by my full name instead of Kiyo or Kiyo-chan, that meant he meant business. He never punched my head once, but I'd seen him slap and punch Tosh's head all over the place till Tosh was black and blue in the head.

"Yes, Father." I was scared.

"Kiyoshi, you're not to eat anymore at Makoto-san's home. You understand?"

"But why, Father? Nobuyuki-san and Mitsunobu-san eat with me too!"

"Nemmind!" he said in English. Then he said in Japanese, "You're not a monkey. You're Kiyoshi Oyama."

"But why?" I said again. I wasn't being smart-alecky like Tosh. I really wanted to know why.

Father grew angry. You could tell by the way his eyes bulged and the way he twisted his mouth. He flew off the handle real easily, like Tosh. He said, "If you keep on asking 'Why? Why?' I'll crack your head *kotsun!*"

Kotsun doesn't mean anything in Japanese. It's just the sound of something hard hitting your head.

"Yeah, slap his head, slap his head!" Tosh said in pidgin Japanese and laughed.

"Shut up! Don't say uncalled-for things!" Father said to Tosh and Tosh shut up and grinned.

Whenever Father talked about this younger generation talking too much and talking out of turn and having no respect for anything, he didn't mean me, he meant Tosh.

"Kiyoshi, you understand, you're not to eat anymore at Makoto's home," Father said evenly, now his anger gone.

I was going to ask "Why?" again but I was afraid. "Yes," I said.

Then Tosh said across the table in pidgin English, which the old folks couldn't understand, "You know why, Kyo?" I never liked the guy, he couldn't even pronounce my name right. "Because his father no work and his mother do all the work, thass why! Ha-ha-ha-ha!"

Father told him to shut up and not to joke at the table and he shut up and grinned.

Then Tosh said again in pidgin English, his mouth full of food; he always talked with his mouth full, "Go tell that *kodomo taisho* to go play with guys his own age, not small shrimps like you. You know why he doan play with us? Because he scared, thass why. He too *wahine*. We bust um up!"

"Wahine" was the Hawaiian word for woman. When we called anybody *wahine* it meant she was a girl or he was a sissy. When Father said *wahine* it meant the old lady or Mother.

Then I made another mistake. I bragged to Tosh about going across the breakers. "You *pupule* ass! You wanna die or what? You want shark to eat you up? Next time you go outside the breakers I goin' slap your head!" he said.

"Not dangerous. Makot been take me go."

"Shaddup! You tell that *kodomo taisho* if I catch um taking you outside the breakers again, I going bust um up! Tell um that! Tell um I said go play with guys his own age!"

"He never been force me. I asked um to take me."

"Shaddup! The next time you go out there, I goin' slap your head!"

Tosh was three years older than me and when he slapped my head, I couldn't slap him back because he would slap me right back, and I couldn't cry like my kid sister because I was too big to cry. All I could do was to walk away mad and think of all the things I was going to do to get even when I grew up. When I slapped my sister's head she would grumble or sometimes cry but she would always talk back, "No slap my head, you! Thass where my brains stay, you know!" Me, I couldn't even talk back. Most big brothers were too cocky anyway and mine was more cocky than most.

Then at supper Tosh brought it up again. He spoke in pidgin Japanese (we spoke four languages: good English in school, pidgin English among ourselves, good or pidgin Japanese to our parents and the other old folks), "Mama, you better tell Kyo not to go outside the breakers. By-'n'-by he drown. By-'n'-by the shark eat um up."

"Oh, Kiyo-chan, did you go outside the breakers?" she said in Japanese.

"Yeah," Tosh answered for me, "Makoto Sasaki been take him go."

"Not dangerous," I said in pidgin Japanese; "Makoto-san was with me all the time."

"Why shouldn't Makoto-san play with people his own age, *ne*?" Mother said.

"He's a *kodomo taisho,* thass why!"

Kodomo taisho meant General of the kids.

"Well, you're not to go outside the breakers anymore. Do you understand, Kiyo-chan?" Mother said.

I turned to Father, who was eating silently. "Is that right, Father?"

"So," he grunted.

"Boy, your father and mother real strict," Makot said. I couldn't go outside the breakers, I couldn't go eat at his place. But Makot always saved some corned beef and onions and Campbell soup for me. He told me to go home and eat fast and just a little bit and come over to his place and eat with them and I kept on doing that without Mother catching on. And Makot was always buying us pie, ice cream, and chow fun, and he was always giving me the biggest share of the pie, ice cream, or chow fun. He also took us to the movies now and then and when he had money for only one treat or when he wanted to take only me and spend the rest of the money on candies, he would have me meet him in town at night, as he didn't want me to come to his place at night. "No tell Mit and Skats," he told me and I didn't tell them or the folks or Tosh anything about it, and when they asked where I was going on the movie nights, I told them I was going over to Mit's or Skats'.

Then near the end of summer the whole town got tired of going to the beach and we all took up slingshots and it got to be slingshot season. Everybody made slingshots and carried pocketsful of little rocks and shot linnets and myna birds and doves. We would even go to the old wharf and shoot the black crabs which crawled on the rocks. Makot made each of us a dandy slingshot out of a guava branch, as he'd made each of us a big barbed spear out of a bedspring coil during spearing-fish season. Nobody our age had slingshots or spears like ours, and of the three he made, mine was always the best. I knew he liked me the best.

Then one day Makot said, "Slingshot waste time. We go buy a rifle. We go buy twenty-two."

"How?" we all said.

Makot said that he could get five dollars from his old folks and all we needed was five dollars more and we could go sell coconuts and mangoes to raise that.

"Sure!" we all said. A rifle was something we saw only in the movies and Sears Roebuck catalogues. Nobody in Pepelau owned a rifle.

So the next morning we got a barley bag, two picks, and a scooter wagon. We were going to try coconuts first because they were easier to sell. There were two bakeries in town and they needed them for coconut pies. The only trouble was that free coconut trees were hard to find. There were trees at the courthouse, the Catholic Church, and in Reverend Hastings' yard, but the only free trees were those deep in the cane fields and they were too tall and dangerous. Makot said, "We go ask Reverend Hastings." Reverend Hastings was a minister of some kind and he lived alone in a big old house in a big weedy yard next to the kindergarten. He had about a dozen trees in his yard and he always let you pick some coconuts if you asked him, but he always said, "Sure, boys, provided you don't sell them." "Aw, what he doan know won't hurt um," Makot said. Makot said he was going to be the brains of the gang and Mit and Skats were going to climb the trees and I was going to ask Reverend Hastings. So we hid the wagon and picks and bags and I went up to the door of the big house and knocked.

Pretty soon there were footsteps and he opened the door. "Yes?" He smiled. He was a short, skinny man who looked very weak and who sort of wobbled when he walked, but he had a nice face and a small voice.

"Reverend Hastings, can we pick some coconuts?" I said.

Makot, Mit and Skats were behind me and he looked at them and said, "Why, sure, boys, provided you don't sell them."

"Thank you, Reverend Hastings," I said, and the others mumbled, "Thank you."

"You're welcome," he said and went back into the house.

Mit and Skats climbed two trees and knocked them down as fast as they could and I stuck my pick in the ground and started peeling them as fast as I could. We were scared. What if he came out again? Maybe it was better if we all climbed and knocked down lots and took them somewhere else to peel them, we said. But Makot sat down on the wagon and laughed, "Naw, he not gonna come out no more. No be chicken!" As soon as he said that the door slammed and we all looked. Mit and Skats stayed on the trees but didn't knock down any more. Reverend Hastings jumped down the steps and came walking across the yard in big angry strides! It was plain we were going to sell the coconuts because we had more than half a bagful and all the husks were piled up like a mountain! He came up, his face red, and he shouted, "I thought you said you weren't going to sell these! Get down from those trees!"

I looked at my feet and Makot put his face in the crook of his arm and began crying, "Wah-wah . . ." though I knew he wasn't crying.

Reverend Hastings grabbed a half-peeled coconut from my hand and grabbing it by a loose husk, threw it with all his might over the fence and nearly fell down and shouted, "Get out! At once!" Then he turned right around and walked back and slammed the door after him.

"Ha-ha-ha!" Makot said as soon as he disappeared, "we got enough anyway."

We picked up the rest of the coconuts and took them to the kindergarten to peel them. We had three dozen and carted them to the two bakeries on Main Street. But they said that they had enough coconuts and that ours were too green and six cents apiece was too much. We pulled the wagon all over town and tried the fish markets and grocery stores for five cents. Finally we went back to the first bakery and sold them for four cents. It took us the whole day and we made only $1.44. By that time Mit, Skats and I wanted to forget about the rifle, but Makot said, "Twenty-two or bust."

The next day we went to the tall trees in the cane fields. We had to crawl through tall cane to get to them and once we climbed the trees and knocked down the coconuts we had to hunt for them in the tall cane again. After the first tree we wanted to quit but Makot wouldn't hear of it and when we didn't move he put on his *habut. Habut* is short for *habuteru,* which means to pout the way girls and children do. Makot would blow up his cheeks like a balloon fish and not talk to us. "I not goin' buy you no more chow fun, no more ice cream, no more pie," he'd sort of cry, and then we would do everything to please him and make him come out of his *habut.* When we finally agreed to do what he wanted he would protest and slap with his wrist like a girl, giggle with his hand over his mouth, talk in the kind of Japanese which only girls use, and in general make fun of the girls. And when he came out of his *habut* he usually bought us chow fun, ice cream, or pie.

So we crawled through more cane fields and climbed more coconut trees. I volunteered to climb too because Mit and Skats grumbled that I got all the easy jobs. By three o'clock we had only half a bag, but we brought them to town and again went all over Main Street trying to sell them. The next day we went to pick mangoes, first at the kindergarten, then at Mango Gulch, but they were harder to sell so we spent more time carting them around town.

"You guys think you so hot, eh" Tosh said one day. "Go sell mangoes and coconuts. He only catching you head. You know why he pick on you guys for a gang? Because you guys the last. That *kodomo taisho* been leader of every shrimp gang and they all quit him one after another. You, Mit, and Skats stick with him because you too stupid!"

I shrugged and walked away. I didn't care. I liked Makot. Besides, all the guys his age were jealous because Makot had so much money to spend.

Then several days later Father called me. He was alone at the outside sink, cleaning some fish. He brought home the best fish for us to eat but it was always fish. He was still in his fisherman's clothes.

"Kiyoshi," he said and he was not angry, "you're not to play with Makoto Sasaki anymore. Do you understand?"

"But why, Father?"

"Because he is bad." He went on cleaning fish.

"But he's not bad. He treats us good! You mean about stealing mangoes from kindergarten? It's not really stealing. Everybody does it."

"But you never sold the mangoes you stole before?"

"No."

"There's a difference between a prank and a crime. Everybody in town is talking about you people. Not about stealing, but about your selling mangoes and coconuts you stole. It's all Makoto's fault. He's older and he should know better but he doesn't. That's why he plays with younger boys. He makes fools out of them. The whole town is talking about what fools he's making out of you and Nobuyuki and Mitsunobu."

"But he's not really making fools out of us, Father. We all agreed to make some money so that we could buy a rifle and own it together. As for the work, he doesn't really force us. He's always buying us things and making things for us and teaching us tricks he learns in Boy Scout, so it's one way we can repay him."

"But he's bad. You're not to play with him. Do you understand?"

"But he's not bad! He treats us real good and me better than Mitsunobu-san or Nobuyuki-san!"

"Kiyoshi, I'm telling you for the last time. Do not play with him."

"But why?"

"Because his home is bad. His father is bad. His mother is bad."

"Why are his father and mother bad?"

"Nemmind!" He was mad now.

"But what about Mitsunobu-san and Nobuyuki-san? I play with them too!"

"Shut up!" He turned to face me. His mouth was twisted. "You're not a monkey! Stop aping others! You are not to play with him! Do you understand! Or do I have to crack your head *kotsun!*"

"Yes," I said and walked away.

Then I went inside the house and asked Mother, "Why are they bad? Because he doesn't work?"

"You're too young to understand, Kiyo-chan. When you grow up you'll know that your parents were right."

"But whom am I going to play with then?"

"Can't you play with Toshi-chan?"

"Yeah, come play with me, Kyo. Any time you want me to bust up that *kodomo taisho* I'll bustum up for you," Tosh said.

That night I said I was going to see Mit and went over to Makot's home. On the way over I kept thinking about what Father and Mother said. There was something funny about Makot's folks. His father was a tall, skinny man and he didn't talk to us kids the way all the other old Japanese men did. He owned a Model T when only the *haoles* or whites had cars. His mother was funnier yet. She wore lipstick in broad daylight, which no other Japanese mother did.

I went into Filipino Camp and I was scared. It was a spooky place, not like Japanese Camp. The Filipinos were all men and there were no women or children and the same-looking houses were all bare, no curtains in the windows or potted plants on the porches. The only way you could tell them apart was by their numbers. But I knew where Makot's house was in the daytime, so I found it easily. It was the only one with curtains and ferns and flowers. There were five men standing in the dark to one side of the house. They wore shoes and bright aloha shirts and sharply pressed pants, and smelled of expensive pomade. They were talking in low voices and a couple of them were jiggling so hard you could hear the jingle of loose change.

I called from the front porch, "Makot! Makot!" I was scared he was going to give me hell for coming at night.

Pretty soon his mother came out. I had never spoken to her though I'd seen her around and knew who she was. She was a fat woman with a fat face, which made her eyes look very small.

"Oh, is Makoto-san home?" I asked in Japanese.

"Makotooooo!" she turned and yelled into the house. She was all dressed up in kimono. Mother made a lot of kimonos for other people but she never had one like her. hers. She had a lot of white powder on her face and two round red spots on her cheeks.

"Oh, Sasaki-san," I said, "I've had lunch at your home quite a few times. I wanted to thank you for it but I didn't have a chance to speak to you before. It was most delicious. Thank you very much."

She stared at me with her mouth open wide and suddenly burst out laughing, covering her mouth and shaking all over, her shoulders, her arms, her cheeks.

Makot came out. "Wha-at?" he pouted in Japanese. Then he saw me and his face lit up, "Hiya, Kiyo, old pal, old pal, what's cookin'?" he said in English.

His mother was still laughing and shaking and pointing at me.

"What happened?" Makot said angrily to his mother.

"That boy! That boy!" She still pointed at me. "Such a nice little boy! Do you know what he said? He said, 'Sasaki-san . . .' " And she started to shake and cough again.

"Aw, shut up, Mother!" Makot said. "Please go inside!" and he practically shoved her to the door.

She turned around again, "But you're such a courteous boy, aren't you? 'It was most delicious. Thank you very much.' A-ha-hahaha. A-hahahaha . . ."

"Shut up, Mother!" Makot shoved her into the doorway. I would never treat my mother like that but then my mother would never act like that. When somebody said, "Thank you for the feast," she always said, "But what was served you was really rubbish."

Makot turned to me, "Well, what you say, old Kiyo, old pal? Wanna go to the movies tonight?"

I shook my head and looked at my feet. "I no can play with you no more."

"Why?"

"My folks said not to."

"But why? We never been do anything bad, eh?"

"No."

"Then why? Because I doan treat you right? I treat you okay?"

"Yeah. I told them you treat me real good."

"Why then?"

"I doan know."

"Aw, hell, you can still play with me. They doan hafta know. What they doan know won't hurt them."

"Naw, I better not. This time it's my father and he means business."

"Aw, doan be chicken, Kiyo. Maybe you doan like to play with me."

"I like to play with you."

"Come, let's go see a movie."

"Naw."

"How about some chow fun. Yum-yum."

"Naw."

"Maybe you doan like me then?"

"I like you."

"You sure?"

"I sure."

"Why then?"

"I doan know. They said something about your father and mother."

"Oh," he said and his face fell and I thought he was going to cry.

"Well, so long, then, Kiyo," he said and went into the house.

"So long," I said and turned and ran out of the spooky camp.

PART II

The Substitute

Mother had always been weak and sickly but she got so sick I thought she was going to die. It was the end of January 1934 and we all had rotten teeth but hers were the worst and she had them all pulled at Dr. Hamaguchi's and fainted and was rushed to Dr. Kawamura's. She stayed at Dr. Kawamura's three-bed hospital for a week and father had to stay home and cook and launder for us as he'd done a year ago for a couple of months. Tosh was a freshman in high school and he went directly to Aoki Store after school, and so I was number one son and father told me to look after things when he decided to go out to sea. I told three-year-old Hanae to look in on mother every so often and come and get me at school if she fainted. Takako and Miwa were in school with me.

We always stopped home after grade school on our way to language school, and after a week mother was on her cushion on the floor, legs doubled under her, sewing a kimono.

"Why don't you rest some more?" I said.

"I'm all right."

"Why don't you sew something easy like a pants or a dress?"

"There's more money in a kimono."

"Why don't you sit on a chair or at the sewing machine where you can stretch your legs?"

"There's a proper way of doing everything."

Father's fishing was so bad, mother's sewing was the only money coming in lots of times. She'd taught herself to sew by watching Mr. Oshiro sew when we lived next door to his tailor shop on Dickenson Street. Both Tosh and I got hit by cars, and mother finally persuaded father that it was a bad-luck house, and we moved to Omiya Camp. Now she took more orders than she could handle.

A couple of weeks later I came home from Liliuokalani School and shouted as usual, *"Tada ima!"* When she didn't answer, I ran into the house without washing my feet. She was sprawled on the floor. "Mother!" I shook her and touched her forehead. I got a *futon* from the bedroom and lifted her onto it and freed her legs

from under her and covered her with another *futon.* Then I flew
out of the house shouting, "Hanae! Hanae!" and kept running.
I met Takako and Miwa coming home from school. "Quick! Taka-
chan, go get Mrs. Kanai! Mama's fainted! Miwa, you stay with
Mama! Hurry! Run!" I didn't stop till I got to Dr. Kawamura's
and my face felt puffed like a balloon fish. "Doctor, mother has
fainted! I just found her! I don't know how long she's been unconscious!"

He grabbed his black bag and drove his car to Back Street and
through the dirt road into Omiya Camp. He knelt beside mother
and put something under her nose and she jerked back her head
and opened her eyes. "I—I felt so dizzy," she said. "You'll be all
right. Can you stand up? We'll take you to the hospital for a
checkup." We lifted her and took her to his car. The three-bed
hospital was empty, and mother said, "I'll take the same bed, it
was lucky the last time," and we lowered her into it. Mrs. Kanai,
the wife of the Methodist language school principal, bustled in
with Takako. "What happened? How are you?" "I'm sorry to be
such a nuisance," mother said. "You're not being a nuisance," she
sat on a chair and held mother's hand. Then she went into the
other room and talked to Dr. Kawamura and came out. "The
doctor says you're going to be all right, your mother's going to be
all right," turning to me and Takako. "Come, Taka-chan, I'll walk
you back to school. Kiyo-chan will sit with her. You have to get
well, *ne?* You have to *want* to get well, *ne?* It would be *zannen* to
die in a strange place like Hawaii, *ne?*"

Father was out at sea and was not due back till tomorrow night.
When Takako came back from her one-hour language school class,
I sent her to Aoki Store to get Tosh. "How you feeling?" Tosh
said. "I'm all right now, I just overworked myself." "You shouldn't
worry about the debt. Just take care of your body." When outside
Tosh said, "How come you never been call me earlier?" "I would've
if she was real bad." "You goin' stay with her?" "Yeah." "Good.
When's Papa coming home?" "Tomorrow." "You know, he oughta
quit fishing. There's no more fish left in the sea. All it does is we
go deeper in the hole and Mama over-worries and overworks. And
damn *wahine,* she too superstitious. She thinks she goin' die, she
believe in it. She talk to you about it?" "No." "Yeah, she no can
get it out of her head." "Why?" "They all like that. Bulaheads are
crazy."

Mother did seem to have more superstitions than most people.
She insisted that rice should always be scooped at least twice from
the big bowl to the individual bowls even if the second scoop was

a token one without any rice on the ladle. The double scooping protected the family from seeing a second mother, meaning your first mother would not die or run away. *Mama* in Japanese meant cooked rice or mother.

Then there was the bad-luck word *shi*. It could be the number "four" or "death" depending on the character. All through 1933 mother worried about father because he was forty-two years old and forty-two was bad luck because it was pronounced *shi-ni*, which had the same sound as *shi-ni-iku* (to go to die). Father laughed it off saying it was nothing but silly Chinese and Buddhist superstition, but sure enough he had two near fatal accidents at sea. Once his anchor rope got tangled around his propeller in a storm and he drifted a full day before he cut it loose. He tied a rope around his waist and dived beneath the boat and dived for his life every time the thirty-two-foot sampan reared up and slapped its stern over his head like a giant palm. The other fishermen had organized a search party by the time he came chugging home. He shrugged, "With the rope, they'd find my body at least." Later in the year a *tsunami* slammed his boat against a pile of rocks near the wharf. The boat was badly damaged, but he escaped without a scratch.

I went home to cook for the girls and went back to the small hospital room and sat there while mother slept. I skipped school the next day and stayed at the hospital. She was awake but didn't seem to get any better.

I sent Miwa to wait for father at the wharf the next day and he came directly to the hospital. "How are you?" "I'm just tired." Mother had a tall nose with a slight cleft at the end. She rubbed it with the tip of her finger like she was trying to rub it smooth, "In Japan they say people with these clefts die young." "Don't talk like a fool, you'll outlive us all," father said.

She stayed at the hospital for three days and father stayed home and cooked and sat with her. When he decided to go out to sea after a week, I was assigned to cook and pack the school lunches and cook supper and build the fire for the bath. Hanae was to watch her and not run off to play as she'd done before. Takako was to help with the cooking and she and Miwa were to wash the dishes and clothes and do the ironing. Every night I cooked some rice gruel and crushed some fried fish with a spoon and tried to feed mother like she was a baby, but she hardly ate. Dr. Kawamura came every day with more pills and medicines in bottles, but they didn't seem to help her.

One day she looked so tired I stayed home from school and sat with her.

"We have a very large debt," she said weakly. "We owe Aoki Store about $2,000, then Chatani Fish Market, hmmm, maybe about the same, Tanabe Store about $400, Saito Store about $200, the rent to Kanagawa about $300, Dr. Hamaguchi the dentist $150, Dr. Kawamura about $300. Except for Aoki Store and Chatani Fish Market you have to pay them at least $5.00 a month to show them you're sincere. There're other smaller debts but I can't remember them now. They're in my record book in the sewing machine drawer. We've been in debt from the very day I came to Hawaii. It's bad luck if you don't pay off your debts by New Year's. That's why maybe . . ."

"Don't worry. Toshi-chan and I shall be out of school soon and working and we'll pay off the debt in no time once we start working."

"It's too bad you're not the number one son. You're wiser than Toshio so you have to see to it that he and father don't fight so much. He's so disrespectful, he says the first thing which comes into his mind and shouts so much he scares the girls. Takako and Miwa aren't as good in school, but Hanae is more like you and Toshio. It's better that way, boys should have better heads. Look after them, they like you, they—"

"Don't tire yourself, save your strength," I felt sick in my stomach.

A couple of days later she said, "You know, there's a saying, 'A bad wife is fifty years of bad crops.' They say fifty years because that's how long the average life was then. I'm thirty-seven now by Japanese age. I wasn't a bad wife, but a bad-luck wife. Funny thing is your father's family asked for me because my grandfather and your father's grandmother were brother and sister. In Japan you investigate the bride's family for insanity, leprosy and other diseases. Being in Hawaii, they couldn't investigate any picture bride so they asked for me whom they knew to be safe, being a relative. I cried when I left, 'Don't worry, father, mother, I'll be back in five years! I'll work hard for my husband's family for four years and everything I earn in the fifth year I'll save for you!' That was in 1915. After that it was all hardship. In 1922 grandfather finally saved enough money to repay his debts in Japan and open his store in Tokyo. The next year the earthquake wiped out everything. Twenty years of work in the cane fields for your grandfather, twelve years for your father, half of that maybe for his two younger brothers. Everything in the first seven years of our marriage was handed over to grandfather. Years of frugal living and saving wiped out in less than a day. That's fate. It can't be helped."

"Rest, don't tire yourself."

"I didn't know what work was till I came to Hawaii. There were only two of us in the family, me and my sister, and father was so gentle. He wasn't any good at farming or business either and he sold his farm like grandfather and went into business and went bankrupt. He wrote me just before he died that he was overjoyed in a way when that letter came from Hawaii in 1914 asking for my hand. He didn't have enough money to give me away in Japan and it had been worrying him how he was going to get me married off and the proposal from Hawaii solved everything. He wasn't strong and he played the stock market and barely supported us, but he spoiled us both. Then he died suddenly of a stroke. No, it wasn't so suddenly. Your youngest uncle graduated from Wakayama University in June and in August he was dead from tuberculosis. He worked his way through college and strained his health. Your grandmother doted on him and she just wasted away and died of grief in November. Then on December 14 father died of a stroke. So it was happening all the time, it's still happening, it happens in cycles of fours. It must be some retribution. What did I do? I lie here and search and search my mind."

"We've never done anything that bad."

"No, but some close relative might've. We can get punished as the substitute."

You heard about Death, but you never saw it. It only happened to grandparents in faraway Japan. Nobody had grandparents in Hawaii. *Obaban* or Granny in Kahana was an exception. She was grandfather's older sister. She was the oldest in the family, but grandfather was number one son. "*Obaban* was black sheep," Tosh explained to me once. "They been kick her out of the family in Japan."

"Why?"

"Because she been elope with *Anshan's* father. Her father been die and she been elope with him before the forty-nine-day mourning period was over. Here you not supposed to even drink *sake* for forty-nine days, and she been run off and marry *Anshan's* father. So the family in Japan kicked her out for good, they cut her off and told her they considered her dead. Thass why she been come to Kahana. She was one of the first ones in Kahana. It was just dirt then, no trees, and she been born six kids with *Anshan's* father. *Anshan* was number six. Then she been ditch *Anshan's* father and marry Kitano. But *Obaban* was the only one who was kind to

Mama when Mama been come from Japan. Everybody, especially Grandma, been treat Mama like dirt. Thass when *Obaban* been step in and save Mama's life. She was older than grandfather so she could tell him off. The Oyama men are kind of gutless and Grandma was a miser and a slavedriver."

"You been know her?"

"No."

"How you know?"

"*Anshan* been tell me. When he was drunk. Not only that, *Obaban* got hot pants. All the Oyamas got hot pants."

"What's 'hot pants'?"

"You doan know what's 'hot pants'?"

"No."

"Forget it then."

I stayed home the next day and about nine she said, "*Obaban* hasn't come to see me. I'd like to see her."

"Shall I go get her?"

"No, it costs too much to hire a taxi all the way to Kahana."

"I can go to Aoki Store and phone the plantation store in Kahana and ask them to ask *Obaban* to come."

"No, it'll just be more trouble."

"She doesn't know you're sick. You should've written her."

"I thought it'd just be a trifle."

"I'll go get her."

"No."

The neighbors and friends of the family had come bringing oranges and fruits in paper sacks, but *Obaban* in far-off Kahana hadn't heard anything. She wouldn't find out unless we told her. She'd been midwife for all of us and when Hanae was born, father woke me up at 4 a.m. to bring *Obaban* in the Mikami taxi. I got to Kahana before five and found *Obaban* in her plantation house packing the day's lunches for Mr. Kitano and *Anshan*. She dropped everything and we rushed back to Pepelau in the taxi. We got back to our house before six and Hanae was born at 8 a.m.

Now the more I thought about it the more nervous I got. It's silly to think money at a time like this. Besides, mother was always denying herself for us, she asked so little for herself it'd be terrible not to give her what little she asked when she did ask. About ten I went into the bedroom and said, "I'm getting the Mikami taxi to bring *Obaban*."

"You shouldn't. She'll come later."

"She doesn't know how sick you are, I mean, she doesn't know you're sick."

"You'll only trouble her."

"She'd be glad to come."

"Thank you," she said weakly.

I had visited *Obaban* for a week every summer. It gave me something new to write about when I went back to school in the fall. Otherwise "What I Did During Summer" would be the same old thing, spearing fish in the morning, surfing in the afternoon, then swimming at the old wharf till sunset. Tosh was working the last two summers so I went alone and I spent a lot of time with *Obaban*. She was real old, so old she could sit cross-legged with the men in the parlor and smoke her long pipe and tell the men off in her low voice. But she sighed a lot and didn't talk much.

She was in the kitchen when I ran in, "*Obaban,* mother is very sick and wants to see you."

"Oh, what happened?"

"She pulled out all her teeth a month ago and fainted and got worse. She can't eat anything. She said she wanted to see you but didn't want to trouble you. I told her the only reason you haven't come is because you didn't know. I got the Mikami taxi waiting. Can you come?"

"Of course. Why didn't somebody tell me?"

"We should've written."

"Where's your father?"

"He's out at sea. He stayed home for a week."

"Where's Toshio?"

"He's in high school, he goes directly to Aoki Store and works till late."

I'd forgotten how cool this mountain village was. Living in Pepelau, you figured every other place was having the same heat spell.

She put on a wide skirt which came to her ankles and a matching blue-grey jacket. She had square jaws and shoulders and wide hips and hobbled slightly. I helped her into the taxi and got into the back with her. "She shouldn't have so many children," she muttered as we rode down the hill toward the sea. "What?" "Nothing," she patted my hand. She always seemed like she was too tired, like it was a strain for her to talk, "Stop it," she'd say every time Mr. Kitano and *Anshan* argued back and forth too much. Even when she sat cross-legged with the men she didn't say much, even when they stopped and asked her opinion she'd say "Hmmm" in her deep voice. She had a black lacquer Buddhist altar on the parlor wall and higher up beside the doorway to the bedroom, a Shinto *kami-dana* shelf. She always burned incense at the Buddhist altar and had food offerings at both. "Why do you put out the food?" I asked her one day when she offered me a star fruit from the altar. "They're for my parents, your great grand-parents." "Do they eat it?" "They eat the spirit of it." "What if you don't put it out?" "Then they get hurt and angry." "Are they ghosts?" "No, they're spirits." "What happens if they get hurt and angry?" "They're like living people, they can harm you like living people." "But what if they can't find you?" She laughed then, the only time I remember her laughing, "That's why we hang paper lanterns during *Bon,* so that they won't get lost."

Once you got back down to the sea the road followed the shoreline. The cane fields came down to the tar road, and on the other side of the road was the narrow strip of sand and the ocean. The island was a mountaintop, and the land sloped from the shore for about five miles to the foot of the bluish-green mountains. Sugar cane covered the entire slope, and the plantation spotted camps like Kahana in the light green fields to farm the fields around them. Kahana sat on the northern slope and it caught a lot of wind and rain. Things grew wild in Kahana, whereas there wasn't enough water in Pepelau even for a home garden.

As Mr. Mikami curved in and out with the shoreline, I said in a low voice, "*Obaban,* do you believe in *bachi*?" (retribution)

"Why?" she said after a while.

"Mother thinks she's getting somebody else's *bachi.*"

"Hmmm."

"She believes she's being punished as somebody else's substitute."

"Hmmm."

"Do you believe that?"

"It can work both ways," she said tiredly. "If she can find another substitute, then she'd be freed."

I watched her for a while fingering one of her amulets. She always carried several of them in her purse. "Can you give mother one of your amulets?"

"Well, all of mine have my name on them, but I can have one made for her at the temple."

"Does it really work?"

"Yes, if you believe it does."

Bachi was a punishment you got when you did something bad and got away with it. The scary part was it didn't have to happen to the wrongdoer himself, it could fall on his children or any substitute. Father pooh-poohed the whole thing, "If you wait long enough, some bad luck is bound to happen to everybody." Father had become a Methodist soon after he came to Hawaii. In the old days there was nothing going on in Kahana on Sundays except at the Methodist Church, he said. When mother was sent for to be his bride, she became a Methodist too and we were all baptized. Father didn't believe in Christianity any more than he did in Buddhism, but mother had grown up in the country steeped in all the superstitions. Most of them had to do with warding off bad luck. Each New Year had to be started clean: all debts paid, all the food cutting and cooking done by midnight on New Year's Eve, there should be no cleaning or sweeping or cooking except rewarming on New Year's Day, and you bathed in the morning on New Year's Day. Then there were all the things having to do with death: if you stumbled on your way to a funeral somebody in your family would die, if you were sleepier than usual a relative would die, if you sliced a melon at night you would not be present when your parent died. I tried to laugh them off like father, but mother worried about them so much she made me worry.

When we walked into the bedroom mother sat up with outstretched arms and in a moment she was clasping *Obaban* and crying like a child. "Come," I took Hanae's hand and led her out. I told Mr. Mikami I'd come and get him at his stand when *Obaban* was ready to go home, and Hanae and I sat on the veranda. "Is Mama goin' die?" She asked. "No." Mother was always fixing fish some new way, saying eating a new dish made you live seventy-five days longer. There would be no more special eats and the kitchen would be cold forever. On nights when father was at sea mother always set the first bowl of rice at his place on the table and talked about all the fish he was catching and how tired he must be. We'd have an early supper at times and walk to the beach and watch the sunset and when it got dark, mother would say, "Good night, father," and we'd all say, "Good night, father," to the ocean. There was a low chanting from the bedroom, sounding at times like a hum. *Obaban* was praying. I'd heard the same kind of chanting when passing Buddhist temples. It was loudest during funerals.

Then she stopped and they were talking and I went in and said from the doorway, "I'll go get your taxi." *Obaban* nodded. "Sorry to cause you so much trouble," mother kept saying. "You'll be all right, I'll make an offering at our altar." I rode back with Mr. Mikami and asked him to charge the fare to the family. "You'll get the amulet for mother?" I said as I helped *Obaban* into the back seat. "Yes." "Thank you, *Obaban*." "You're a good boy," she patted the back of my hand. Nothing else had worked, none of my prayers, none of Dr. Kawamura's medicines.

Mother looked relaxed. "How about some gruel?"

"No, I'm not hungry."

"You're really fond of *Obaban.*"

"She's my Hawaiian mother. I didn't even have a wedding ring when I got married. She made me one out of a gold coin. See?" It was the band she always wore.

"I understand grandmother was very mean to you."

"She couldn't help it. She had such a hard life herself."

"Why didn't father protect you?"

"How could he? He had to be a filial son first."

"Why do the Buddhists have a forty-nine day mourning period?"

"That's how long it takes the dead spirit to tidy up everything on earth."

"Where does it go then?"

"Depends, but most of them go to Amida's paradise."

"Why is it so bad for the relatives to act differently during the forty-nine days?"

"They shouldn't disturb the dead spirit while it's making its preparations to leave."

"Is that why they have *hi no tama*?" (fireballs) These were bluish fireballs the size of a softball, which hovered late at night around the eaves of a house in which there had been a death. Everybody talked about it, but nobody saw one.

"Hmmm, they say it's a sign of a disturbed spirit."

"Have you seen one?"

"No."

"Why don't you go to sleep?"

"Yes."

She slept for several hours and when she got up about three, she said, "I had a marvelous dream. I was back in Japan and father was still alive and we all cuddled and cried. You know, I was sent for as your father's bride so that I could help grandmother with her housework. She'd been cooking, laundering, doing everything for your grandfather, your father and your two uncles who all worked in the cane fields. She kept a dozen pigs, made beancake and pushed her cart around camp to sell them, and she exhausted her body and just couldn't get well. When I got here, your aunt, Masako, who was only four then, said to grandmother, 'Mother, you can die now, elder sister has come from Japan to look after me.' Aren't children terrible?"

"You shouldn't talk so much, you'll tire yourself."

When father came home from sea at dusk I told him he should stay home the next few days. Mother had that look about her I'd taken for relaxation. It was more like *Obaban's* resigned look. She was putting everything in order, she'd said everything she had to say, she'd told you where she kept everything so that she wouldn't be a bother after she left. "She thinks she's been chosen for someone else's punishment," I said. "That's silly superstition," father said, but he stayed home and the next morning I went to school.

About eleven o'clock father showed up at the doorway of my sixth grade class and my heart started pounding like a fist against my chest. He never came except on parents' visiting day when he happened to be home! "Kiyoshi," Mrs. Mikimoto, our teacher, looked suddenly very sad, "there's been a . . . some sad news, you may be excused from class . ." "Please God, please God, please God, let her have a little breath left!" I was shaking all over and wobbling like a drunk as I walked to the head of the class where father waited. *"Baban chubu ni kakatta,"* he whispered, and suddenly I felt like jumping and shrieking like I hit a home run! I had to hold myself now to keep from dancing. *"Baban* had a stroke." "When?" "Ten this morning. They telephoned Aoki Store. I'm going ahead. She might still be alive. You get Takako, Miwa, and Toshio." "Yes." I grabbed his hand and pumped it and he looked at me like I was crazy.

I got Takako and Miwa from their classes and went home. Mother and Hanae were already dressed, and mother was packing some fresh clothes into the old suitcase. She was trembling.

"You shouldn't go, mother, you're still not well," I said.

"I'm all right. I'd insist on being carried if I couldn't walk."

When Mr. Mikami came back from Kahana, I rode with him to Pepelau High which sat a mile above the town and got Tosh. Tosh changed his clothes and we all got in the taxi.

"Don't stumble now," mother warned, and I carried the suitcase and made sure Hanae or Miwa didn't stumble. I felt so relieved I felt kind of guilty. But *Obaban* was the logical substitute, she was old and lived a full life, Mr. Kitano and *Anshan* who was about thirty wouldn't miss her that much. Mrs. Kanai once told us a story in language school of a famous poet who'd been invited to a Name Day and asked to compose a poem. He wrote, *"Jiji ga shine, oya ga shine, ko ga shine."* (The grandfather should die, then the father, and then the son.) His host shouted, "How dare you speak of death when we're celebrating birth!" The poet said, "It celebrates happiness. It's a happy household where death happens chronologically." Things will be looking up now that *Obaban's* put an end to the cycle of bad luck.

When we got to *Obaban's* house in the middle of Japanese

Camp, she was already dead and everybody was mad at everybody else. *Anshan* wanted her cremated so that he could take her ashes with him, Mr. Kitano wanted her buried at the Kahana graveyard in the cane field. Father stepped in and told *Anshan* why didn't he agree with his stepfather for now and afterwards, meaning after Mr. Kitano died, he could dig up *Obaban's* bones and cremate them. Both agreed. Father was a good middle man, but he was angry too. Mr. Komai, the Shingon Buddhist priest, had shown up in his priest's robes as he did at nearly every death or near-death of a Buddhist. "What's he doing here? *Obaban* doesn't belong to his sect," father said. A neighbor said, "Let him pray as long as he's here." Reverend Komai had chanted over the unconscious *Obaban.* When he finished his prayers and clapped his hands, *Obaban* started. "There, she's getting better already," Reverend Komai said. "Fool!" father yelled at him as *Obaban* started to die. "Pay him the money and get him out of here! That's all he comes for anyway!" father said. It wasn't required, but it was understood that Reverend Komai got a ten-dollar bill in a white envelope for his prayers. I felt good that father was the way he was. I'd be a nervous wreck if he was like mother. Here I was acting worse than mother, I'd assumed *Obaban* was dead, I'd wanted her dead, just to be mother's substitute.

Whenever I visited *Obaban* I slept with *Anshan* on the *futon* on the wooden floor in the parlor, and the place always smelled of incense and *Anshan's* Stacomb. Now *Obaban* was laid on the bedroom floor where she and Mr. Kitano slept. She wore a white linen kimono folded left-handed and tied at the waist with a narrow white band. I'd expected to see the kimono on her inside out. "You're wearing your kimono dead-man's style!" mother would scold us whenever we put one on inside out by accident. She must've made that one up. It seemed so strange, here she was not full of life but very alive yesterday. I touched her hand when I thought nobody was looking and shivered at its coldness. This was the first time I was seeing a dead person. We sat on *futons* across the length of *Obaban,* Mr. Kitano and *Anshan* at her head, then father, Tosh, me, mother, Takako, Miwa, and Hanae at her feet. *Obaban* lay between us and the bedroom doorway for which there was no door, and the villagers came in one or two at a time and said the usual polite things except for Mr. Takeshita who came about eight and really let go. "Why, oh, why did you leave us, Kitano-san? Why didn't you wait a little longer? Why didn't you give us a chance to repay you for all the wonderful things you've done for us? Kahana will never be the same without you!" he went on and on, crying real tears and rocking back and forth. He was real old too, and maybe he was thinking of himself. The parlor behind him was filling up with other guests when he finally stopped and wiped his tears and blew his nose like a loud horn, and backed out of the bedroom. I knew then it hadn't been for real. You couldn't turn it off just like that.

Mother sat to my right rocking back and forth, tears streaming down her sunken cheek. She'd try to choke her sobs and she'd gag and burst out crying. I kept looking sideways at her, hoping she'd stop. *Anshan* too was crying buckets. During the short moments when there was no visitor, he'd cry out unable to keep his voice from cracking, "Toshio, Kiyoshi, *Obaban's* gone! We can't visit with her anymore! She's left us!" I didn't feel any real grief but I felt pretty bad for having felt so happy. *Anshan* or *ani-san* (elder brother) was *Obaban's* youngest child by her first marriage. In a Japanese divorce all the children go with the father so as not to interfere with the mother's new marriage, and *Anshan's* father had taken them all back to Japan, but *Anshan* was the only one to come back to Hawaii. He loved Johnnie Walker and remembered a lot when drunk, "Ooooooo," sounding like a distant train whistle, "you'll never know, Kiyoshi, how much I suffered. I was only ten and my father farmed me to a carpenter as an apprentice. Ooooo, he was harsh. If I was slow or made a mistake, *kotsun!* right on the head with his wooden plane. Feel this bump? Plantation work is nothing compared to what I went through. I lived and worked for ten years for this man for nothing, not even a cent. But he made me the best carpenter in Hawaii. See this arm? It's crooked and broken at the elbow, but it can hang the best door in all Hawaii. Oooooo, how I suffered. Your mother, too, ooooooo, how she suffered! Your grandmother worked her like a slave, sunrise to way past sunset, seven days a week. But she didn't complain, she did everything she was asked to do when most women would've run away. You look all over Hawaii and you'll not find a woman like your mother." "Why did you come back to Hawaii?" I said. "I wanted to look after *Baban* especially after her death. I knew the worthless Kitano wouldn't do it."

We sat there till about ten, and mother and the girls went to the Nakamura's to spend the night, and Tosh and I went to sleep at another friend's. "*Anshan* taking it real hard, eh?" Tosh said. "Mama too." "It's the last time we goin' visit *Obaban's* house," Tosh said. "Yeah." Mr. Kitano would never invite us. Even *Anshan* would be leaving as soon as the forty-nine days of mourning were over. But I was numb and tired and didn't feel like talking.

The next day I put on a long-sleeve white shirt and tie, a pair of navy blue pants, and my Keds basketball shoes. There were over a dozen women in white aprons at *Obaban's* house, fixing all kinds of meatless eats for after the funeral. They seemed more energetic, brighter faced, less sunburned than the women in Pepelau. I took off my shoes and went into the parlor and peeked into the bedroom, half expecting to see *Obaban* sitting there on a straw mat, smoking her Japanese pipe, the tobacco box with its tin-can ash tray beside her. Last night had been a dream, but now in the bright morning light she was nowhere, like she'd run off for good.

I went back into the yard. A light rain had fallen in the night and the trees danced in the wind. It was what I enjoyed most visiting *Obaban,* fooling around in the green-green yard early in the morning. I'd already be in the ocean with goggle and spear back in Pepelau. But here it was so cold I needed a sweatshirt. I used to climb the mango tree, pick avocados with the long bamboo pole, pick papaya, lime, soursap, starfruit and pomegranate. I picked and ate a chili pepper on my first visit and went crying to *Obaban.* These were *Obaban's* trees and she watered them, fed them manure, and mumbled to them. But I wouldn't hesitate a second if it was a choice between her and mother. Children who lost a parent stuck closer together, but it was more like they were huddling closer waiting for it to strike again. They never got over that dread.

When mother and the girls showed up, I greeted them at the front gate.

"I'm so glad you went to get *Obaban.* We must've both known, something must've told us we wouldn't see her again. It would've been too much if she too died without my seeing her. Thank you, thank you," she held my hand in both of hers and bowed and bowed. Her bony face looked fresh like the air washed by rain.

"She was your substitute."

"I'm such a nobody and twice I've been saved."

She let go my hand and started up the slight hill to join the other women. She walked very slowly, but her steps seemed surer. She wasn't trembling. She paused and put her hand to her mouth, "I feel so ugly. It's been like losing all your old friends at once."

"You'll have to get some false teeth," I said.

"Yes."

PART III

All I Asking For Is My Body

1

On August 1, 1936, another girl was born and father must've been a little disappointed. He named her *Tsuneko* (Common child). By the end of the month he decided to quit fishing and move the family back to Kahana where he'd first arrived in 1910. Tosh was to quit high school and work in the cane fields to help support the family. It was what every number one son was expected to do. Father had done it for twelve years, turning over his entire pay to grandfather every month. Even after mother was sent for in 1915 and even after Tosh was born in 1919, father gave grandfather all of his pay. It was a model story of filial piety, which mother told over and over. Great grandfather died while grandfather was in business college, and grandfather quit school and returned to the family farm in Wakayama, Japan. He was number one son and he inherited the farm, but he wasn't any good at farming and after a couple of years, he sold the farm. He married grandmother who was a couple of years older for her dowry, and he opened a clothing store in Osaka with the dowry and money from the farm. The store kept failing and he kept borrowing money from relatives and friends till he finally went broke seven years later. By then he had a huge debt and three young sons, father being number one. But he refused to declare bankruptcy, and promised every creditor he'd pay back every cent. He looked up *Obaban*, his older sister who'd been kicked out of the family, and wrote to her in Kahana. He left his children with relatives in Japan and came to Kahana in 1902 with grandmother. Three more children were born, and father and his two brothers were sent for, and sent to work in the cane fields. When grandfather finally saved enough money to return to Japan in 1922, mother begged him to leave father and her some money. She was carrying another child, and they had nothing to live on for the next month. Grandfather wept and he begged mother not to ask. He needed every penny he'd saved. He had all the debts he had to pay back in Japan, he had a family of two girls and one boy he was taking back with him. There were the boat fare, winter clothing and a hundred unforeseen expenses after which he had to have enough to open a clothing store in Tokyo. Not only that, he asked father to pay the bill for his fare-well party, which came to $300; he asked father to look after his two younger brothers. He cried, "I'll repay you, I'll send for you as soon as I'm successful! I can't ask for more filial children!" "That's why," mother would say to us, "our minds are at peace even if he should die tomorrow. We've done our filial duty to him."

Moving to Kahana was a shock. The place had no indoor toilets, no private baths. It's what I hated most when I visited *Obaban* in the summer. I went with Mr. Hida of Hida Store in Pepelau, who drove there every Wednesday to deliver the orders he'd taken the week before. If I missed him, it meant I'd be stuck for a whole week. Now I was going to be stuck forever! Where I'd been only three blocks from the ocean in Pepelau, Kahana was two miles from the ocean up a pretty steep hill. In Pepelau the cane fields started beyond the plantation camps of Mill Camp, Ohia Camp, and Hau Camp, a good two miles from the center of town; in Kahana the cane fields surrounded you and they began right beyond your yard. It was like my childhood was chopped off clean.

In Pepelau we called the guys *bobora* (country bumpkins) who were too Japanese. In Kahana everybody was a *bobora*. Their heads looked bigger with their shorter haircuts. Most of the Japa-nese in Kahana had come there in the 1890's and 1900's from farming villages in Japan, and they were cut off from the world ever since. There were many different races in Pepelau, but Kahana had about one hundred Japanese families, about two hundred Filipino men, about seven Portuguese and Spanish families, and only two *haoles*. Mr. Boyle was the principal of the Kahana Grade School, and Mr. Nelson was the overseer of Kahana. There'd been many Chinese workers before, but they left and opened stores in Pepelau and the other towns as soon as their contracts expired.

It was a company town with identical company houses and outhouses, and it was set up like a pyramid. At the tip was Mr. Nelson, then the Portuguese, Spanish, and nisei *lunas* in their nicer-looking homes, then the identical wooden frame houses of Japa-nese Camp, then the more run-down Filipino Camp. There were a plantation store, a plantation mess hall for the Filipino bachelors, a plantation community bathhouse, and a plantation social hall. The *lunas* or strawbosses had their own baths and indoor toilets. There were a Catholic Church, the Japanese language school which became the Methodist Church on Sundays, a Buddhist hall, and a plantation dispensary which was open from 11 to 12 noon every working day.

The macadamized or "government" road ended in front of Mr. Nelson's big yard, and all the roads in camp were "plantation" roads, and the dirt was so red it stained your clothes and feet. The guys in Pepelau used to joke about how they could spot a guy from Kahana by his red feet. The place was so country they used newspaper for toilet paper, and each outhouse building was partitioned into four toilets. The rough one-by-sixteen planks used for the partitions did not go up to the rafters, and you could hear all the farts and everything going on in the other toilets. A three-foot-deep concrete ditch ran underneath all the toilets, and you sat back to back against a common partition with one of the other toilets. You were so close in fact you could touch the other guy's ass if you lifted the big square toilet seat. There were half a dozen rows of outhouses and the ditches under them were flushed downhill to a big concrete irrigation ditch which ran around the lower boundary of the camp, and sooner or later shit, newspaper and all ended up in the furrows of the fields below. The plantation had built pigpens along the four-foot-wide *kukai* ditch, and rented them to the workers. Every family kept pigs.

The house we moved into, No. 173, was the last house on "Pig Pen Avenue" and next to the pigpens and ditch, and when the wind stopped blowing or when the warm Kona wind blew from the south, our house smelled like both an outhouse and a pigpen. Worse yet, the family debt was now $6,000, and the average plantation pay for forty-eight hours a week was $25 a month for adults. There was no sick pay, no holiday pay though you got off Christmas, New Year's, and one day during the County Fair in October.

I felt sorry for Tosh the first few months. He'd come home from the fields and collapse on the wooden floor in the parlor. A couple of times he skipped supper and bath, and slept right through in his denim work clothes covered with dust and stained with red sweat. The work clothes got so red and dirty, mother had to boil them for several hours on Saturdays. She'd done the same thing back in 1915 when she arrived from Japan.

2

"How come you bear more children than you can send to high school?" Tosh said one day when he came home from work.

"You *ni ga haru* (too big for your breeches). You've worked only three months and you're talking big. Look at Minoru Tanaka, Hideo Shimada, Kenji Watanabe, Toru Minami, they've been working for their parents for over ten years, and they never complain," mother said.

"They're dumb, that's why. They don't want to go to high school. With me it's different. I *like* school."

"Every child must repay his parents."

"How much? How long?"

"Your father helped grandfather for twelve years without one word of complaint."

"Grandfather is a thief."

"Don't you dare say that in front of father."

"He had you and father and two uncles work for him for twelve years and he took all the money and ran away to Japan."

"He's an honest man. He wanted to pay back all his debts. He needed all the money to open another store."

"That's why he lost everything. It was his retribution."

"Nobody could've foreseen the earthquake."

"So now you want us to throw away our lives to get papa out of debt."

"Don't worry, we won't depend on you. There's Kiyoshi to help us."

"That's what you get for bearing nothing but good-for-nothing girls."

"You've worked only three months and you're acting like a crybaby."

"I can think ahead, that's why. You and papa can't see beyond your noses."

"We'll depend on Kiyoshi."

They went round and round. Mother was getting stronger now and she didn't give up easy.

Tosh had been a boxing nut from way back. He'd gone to all of the boxing matches at the stadium behind the mill in Pepelau. He hung around the Filipino boxers and watched them train in the empty houses around Pepelau, and he always volunteered whenever they staged a match for the kids. He'd ordered a set of cloth boxing gloves from Sears Roebuck in Los Angeles when we were in Pepelau. Now he ordered a leather set, 18-ounce, and a light bag, which he installed at the back of the house. Every day after work he'd punch it and he could hit it so fast it sounded like a piece of paper caught in an electric fan. And he took me in the back yard and he practiced all the parries and counters shown in Jimmy DeForest's *How to Box* pamphlets. He'd have me lead each time, a left jab, left hook, right cross, and he'd counter. We'd go through it in slow motion first, then gradually pick up speed till he was doing it by reflex almost.

3

In March 1937 the 1,100 Filipino workers on the Frontier Mill Plantation went on strike. Mr. Nelson came to Kahana Grade School and recruited all the seventh and eighth graders to work as weeders from 2:30 till 6:30. We'd all been working Saturdays and Sundays from 5:45 till 1:30 for 65 cents for seven hours. Now the plantation offered us 65 cents for four hours.

The plantation kicked out the 150 or so Filipino strikers from Kahana, and dumped their belongings onto the macadamized road which was county property. None of the strikers could trespass into plantation property. The plantation posted guards armed with revolvers at every dirt road leading into Kahana. The *nisei* and Portuguese guards played cards all day and all night in their tents for $5 a day.

Most of the Filipinos worked as cane cutters and loaders during harvesting season, and they asked for 25 cents a ton for the loaders, and for the cutters 12 cents for 30 feet of thick cane and 10 cents for 30 feet of thin cane. Pay was by production. The strike had started several weeks earlier on the other side of the island; it started out as a strike of the loaders and cutters. They asked the plantation to send them back to the Philippines if they couldn't pay them the new rates.

So every day after school we'd go home and change into denim pants and shirts and report to the plantation office with our hoes. We quit going to language school for the duration of the strike. On Saturdays and Sundays, several of us older bigger boys were sent to irrigate the fields, and the rates were so high we were making $2 a day!

Everybody was happy except our eighth grade teacher. Mr. Snook was a newcomer to the islands. He was a tall thin funny-looking guy with red hair, a long beaklike nose, light horn-rimmed glasses, and a short upper lip which made him look like he was grinning all the time. He slouched and mumbled when he talked, hardly moving his lips. It was hard to take Snooky seriously.

"Boo," he'd mumble, "why are you people so passive? Why do you just sit there and believe everything I say? Why don't you call me a liar? Boo. Wake up. All through life it's going to be the same story over and over. It's going to be one dictator after another. Boo," and everybody would laugh nervously. There were eighteen in the class, a Portuguese girl, two Filipino boys, fourteen Japanese, and Clarence Nelson, the son of the overseer of Kahana Camp. He lived in a big house next to the school. It was the biggest house in camp and its yard was bigger than the school yard. The plantation provided them a full-time yardman and maid.

Snooky said one day, "I'm shocked. I've never seen the likes of it till I came to this paradise of the Pacific."

He shuffled back and forth his shoulders hunched and peered through his thick glasses and mumbled as if talking to himself, "And it's not because I've been sheltered. I waited in the breadlines in Detroit, I rode the rails, I shoveled potash in the Mojave Desert with a fellow traveler who had a PhD, but this is the first time I've seen the likes of it. Ray Stannard Baker called this the last surviving vestige of feudalism in the United States. He was absolutely right. The plantation divides and rules, and you the exploited are perfectly happy to be divided and ruled. Do you see what I'm driving at? The Filipinos strike, and you are all too happy to break that strike. It's a big deal. The plantation raises your pay. Doesn't it prick your conscience just a little bit? Don't you feel you're cutting off your own nose? Or do you feel your nose has nothing to do with your face? Huh?"

"No," Tubby said. "It give me chance to make some money."

"But can't you see it's being done at another's expense? Haven't you heard, 'I am my brother's keeper'? 'We hang together or we hang alone'? Hmmm? Kiyoshi?"

"The point is the Filipinos don't want anybody else to join them. They ask a raise only for themselves. They not mad at us. They mad only at other Filipinos who scab, not us. We not scabs to them," I said.

"Why do they think like that?" he mumbled.

"I don't know. Ask them," I said.

"And you feel no guilt about scabbing?"

"In the first place it's not scabbing, and yes, in the second place I like to make $2 a day," I said.

"Amazing," he mumbled. "Unnerving. This is an education for me, let me tell you. I always thought everybody low on the pecking order hated it. Not so. Not you. You love getting pecked from above, you enjoy pecking those below. Amazing. No wonder you're like stone. Too much pecking order makes for timid individuals. What do you want to be in life? A pecker in the pecking order? A cog in the machine? An eternal yes man? Hmmm? If your answer is yes, then you don't need your brains, and it's senseless for me to stand up here and try to prod you into developing an inquisitive mind."

"What's wrong with pecking order?" Tubby Takeshita said. He was a number one son and had six younger brothers. Most number one sons had that special cockiness about them, no matter how young they were. Tubby's father was real proud that he had seven healthy sons. He'd more than paid his family debt to his ancestors with seven boys to carry on the family line. On top of that he made all his sons promise they'd never leave Kahana even after he died because he would feel lonely if they left. He was twenty years older than his wife.

"What's right with it?" Snooky asked.

"It teach everybody to know his place. It make everything run smooth," Tubby said.

"That's true. It makes trains run on schedule. It's efficient in making money and winning wars."

"What's wrong with making money?" Tubby said.

"Nothing. Nearly everybody does it. Preferably out of someone else's sweat or misfortune. But is that all there is to life? Efficiency and making money? Getting rich efficiently? Becoming a cog in a money-making machine?"

"What else is there?" Tubby said.

"What about fresh air and freedom for the individual? What about standing on your own feet? What about thinking for yourself, using your own noodle. Huh?"

"What's freedom?" Tubby said.

"Freedom means not being part of a pecking order. Freedom means being your own boss," Snooky said.

"Freedom means being a plantation boss," I said.

Everybody laughed.

"What happens," Snooky said, "if you're at the bottom of the pecking order and you're getting a raw deal?"

"You gotta stick together even more if you the underdog," Tubby said.

"How much together? Filipino labor, period? Japanese labor, period? Or all labor? Hmmm? And when do you stop being an underdog and become a top dog, hmmm? Are you underdogs to the Filipinos, hmmm?"

The next day Mr. Nelson walked into the classroom in his breeches and boots and safari hat and sat in the back of the class for an hour. Snooky turned beet red and mumbled hello and cleared his throat several times and said, "Well, now, who can give me an example of a dangling participle and tell me why it dangles? Hmmm? Kiyoshi?"

When Mr. Nelson left, Snooky grinned, "Well-well-well. Well!" turning even redder.

He forgot about dangling participles and grammar for the re-

maining couple of months of school, and kept hammering away at
one thing, "What are the primary virtues? What are the virtues
which are independent, which can't be used for any good or evil
ends? Hmmm?" This was his first year in Hawaii and he lived at
Matsuda Hotel in Pepelau and drove an old jalopy to Kahana every
day. He asked every one of us over and over. ". . . Hmmm, Kiyoshi?"

I'd run out of answers, "Loving your enemy, forgiving seventy
times seven." They were only words like the answer to a homework question, but Reverend Sherman had repeated them so often
they stuck in your head.

"We're discussing fact, not fiction," Snooky mumbled and
everybody laughed.

Tubby Takeshita was a real *hobora* type and he kept coming
back, "The best ones are filial piety, patience, knowing your place,
loyalty, knowing your duty, hard work, guts."

"Hmmm . . . let's see. What if Francisco Franco were your
father . . . ?"

"Who?"

"O.K., let's say, Al Capone were your father. You're filial, obe-
dient, loyal, dutiful, et cetera. Are you a good man? You could be
one of his most dependable, courageous, hard-working gunmen,
ratatat! You're a good man to good old Al, but are you a good
man? I'm asking for virtues which can't be used for bad ends."

"They still the best virtues, because Al Capone can't be your
father," Tubby said.

"What if he were?"

"But he not!"

"All right, Tatsuo, what if your father were John Baldwin, the
manager of Frontier Mill?"

"Sure, I obey him. I obey him now."

"Hmmm . . . o.k. What if your father were one of the Filipinos
on strike?"

"Then I obey him."

"So you have no beliefs beyond obeying your immediate supe-
rior?"

"Yes."

"Yes, you do?"

"Yes, I don't."

"Hmmm. It's the same story over and over. If you make too big
a thing of the secondary virtues, you miss the larger picture. What
is this larger picture? What is the cornerstone of all the virtues?
Hmmm. Michie?"

"Kindness," Michie Kutsunai said.

"Yes, that's an independent virtue. What else, Kiyoshi?"

"Honesty."

"Yes, you can't use honesty for any bad purpose. But what's the queen of virtues?"

He'd walk back and forth in front of the class, and every so often when he was farthest away from Clarence Nelson, he'd mutter under his breath so that only those nearest him could hear, "I just can't get over it, that scabs should be so young, innocent, and angelic," or "Am I my brother's scab?"

When I told him about Snooky, Tosh said, "He a Communist or or a queer. Nice *haoles* always after something else."

I felt sad when school ended, even when I won the DAR medal. I wouldn't be seeing Snooky anymore. He was not coming back next year to Kahana or Hawaii. He was so different from any teacher I've had, *haole,* Oriental, or Hawaiian. He brought up a dozen of his books from Pepelau, and gave them to me when he said goodbye.

I worked as a full-time *hanawai* (irrigation) man the day after graduation. Father had the same job too, though he was contracted with several others, to the C-1 and C-2 fields *makai* of the camp, which caught all the shit and newspapers from the sewage. It was the same job he had when he left Kahana in 1922, though his fields then were B-4 and B-5. The strike was still on and we were sent to irrigate the fields which were drying up and we worked ten hours a day seven days a week. The contract *hanawai* men were paid $1.25 a day, plus so many cents a ton after the cane was harvested twenty-four months later. The plantation paid us by the number of acres four or five of us irrigated as a team, and if we worked hard we could make $2 a day, which was unheard of for a fourteen-year-old.

The strikers looked like a ragged army of stragglers. They set up tents along the government road along the shore. They couldn't build any fires because the plantation had the fire department put a stop to that. The police arrested the leader, Delphin Reyes, and his two helpers and threw them in the prison in Wainae. They were accused of beating up a Filipino scab. The strikers couldn't raise the $200 bail set for each of them.

"The Filipinos are to be pitied. They're running out of food," Tosh said at supper one night.

"They can't win," father said.

"The Japanese should've joined them," Tosh said.

"The Japanese went on strike in 1920 and 1922 and both times the others were the strikebreakers," father said.

"That's why nobody can beat the plantation," Tosh said.

"We shouldn't worry about other people's business," mother said.

"It's our business too," Tosh said. "We fighting the same plantation."

"We should know our place and not anger them. That's the only way we'll gain their respect," father said.

"That's the trouble with the Japanese, they're yellow balls. You don't gain respect by *boto boto*. You gain respect by fighting. We have to fight them. But first we must forget about returning to Japan. We have to cut off all our ties with Japan and become American. That's what Kuroda says too."

"Kuroda is a radical," father said. Kuroda was the editor of the bilingual *Hawaii Daily* in Honolulu.

"Oh, yeah, Hara is a coward," Tosh said. Hara was the editor of the other bilingual, *Nichi Bei Times*. We took the latter.

"It's because of upstarts like Kuroda who don't know their place that the *haoles* hate the Japanese," father said.

"They might hate Kuroda, but they despise people like Hara. By the way, are Kiyo and I registered as Japanese citizens?"

Father nodded, "It is automatic. Everybody born before 1924 is registered in Japan."

"We want you to cancel ours," Tosh said.

"Is that what *you* want?" mother said to me.

"Yes."

"It'll make it very difficult if you go to Japan," she said.

"I don't want to go to Japan," I said.

"But it doesn't hurt to have both," mother said.

"Yes, it does. We have to choose," Tosh said. "In case of war, Kiyo and me will fight for America."

"It'll never happen," father said.

"Will you cancel them anyway?" Tosh said. "If you don't, I will."

"It's not really necessary," mother said.

"It is necessary," Tosh said. "Will you take ours out?"

Father nodded.

A couple of weeks later Tosh asked him if he'd written to the Japanese consul in Honolulu. Father said yes.

The strike ended in July. The plantation crushed the union and blacklisted its leaders; the strikers got nothing they asked for. The *Hawaii Weekly* said that the strikers admitted that it was a misunderstanding concerning the rates of payment rather than any real dissatisfaction that had caused the strike. After the strike the plantation cut down all the rates they were paying during the strike. The loaders got 25 cents a ton during the strike or what the strikers were asking for. After the strike it went back to 22 cents, and the days when a fourteen-year-old could make $2 a day irrigating was *pau*.

4

The dust hangs in reddish clouds all around us. We are drenched, our denim pants cling to our wet legs, sweat trickles down faces and necks and moistens palms and backs of hands. We wipe continually, hands on pants, shirt sleeves over eyebrows, blue handkerchief around neck. You wear a broad straw hat against the sun, you hold your breath and try to breathe the less dusty air in gasps, you tie the bottom of your pants legs to keep the dust and centipedes out, you stop and clean your nostrils of chocolate dust with the blue handkerchief wet from wiping your neck. Life is fifteen minutes for breakfast, thirty minutes for lunch, *pau hana* at 2:30. It's waiting for Sundays, the County Fair in October when you got a day off, Christmas when there was a program at the language school Methodist Church, New Year's Eve when the Kahana Young People's Association had a dance, and New Year's when all the Japanese homes put out their best eats and anybody could get drunk. The Filipinos' big day was December 30, Rizal Day.

Lino comes to the next furrow. He steps on his shovel. "Jesus Maria!" he says and flings down the shovel and grabs the pick.

"Weee-ha!" Three-Quarter Dalmatio several furrows away shrieks and chants in falsetto, *"Ichiricchi ali bam bam, salagitto a sala bu bam, ama ba yet talan tan tan . . ."* He shovels faster and faster chanting louder. Everybody stops and laughs. "Weeee-ha!" somebody says. "Weee-ha!" another yells louder. Dalmatio chants gasping and flails shovel and red dust into the still air. He's fifty-five, wizened, always working bareback. He works like a madman, in fits of chants, almost jumping up and down, then he lays off the next day.

"Jesus Maria Josep!" Philemon shouts and throws back his head and brays. "Weee-ha! Weee-ha!" he laughs so hard he falls to the ground.

"Jesus Maria! *Ka yot* Philemon!" Awai shouts and throws down his pick and lights a cigarette.

"Weee-ha! Kanaka *loi loi buang buang!*" Philemon shouts, lying on the furrow bank.

"Los los, Philemon! *Yot yot* Philemon!" Awai outshouts Philemon.

Philemon gets up on his shaky legs and lets out a wild "Weeee-ha!" and falls down again.

"Los los you bastards!" Awai says and slams his cigarette to the ground. "The fucking sun too hot! *Yot yot* the sun!"

"Whassa matta, you Awai, you all time *yot yot,* no nuff *yot?*"

Lino says unsure of his English.

"Whassa matta with you, sick or what?" Awai says. "Me not like you and Philemon, don't know how to *yot yot,*" he jerks his hips back and forth.

"Weeee-ha!" Philemon says.

The *luna* (straw boss) comes over and tells Philemon, "You no pock around too much. Bye 'n' bye the beeg boss come."

Philemon sighs and picks himself up, and in a second he's swinging his pick into the caked ground and shoveling chunks of dirt onto the bank. He's a six-footer and he works harder and faster than anybody else in the gang.

"Eassy, eassy, all right," Awai watches Philemon, "take care the body. You work too hard, bye 'n' bye, the plantation cut down the price. Use your *cabeza.*"

Philemon says out of breath, "Nemmind, you like make money, eh?"

"You *loco,* you watch tomorrow, they cut down the price."

"Nemmind," irritably.

During lunch and after work and on days when the whole gang loafs, Awai picks on Philemon. He would hit the bigger Philemon on the arm, wrestle him, and jump on him and pump his hips like Philemon was a woman. Then Philemon would get mad and chase Awai around the cane field and the whole gang would laugh.

"Take care the body," Awai tips his hat and leans on his shovel. He's Hawaiian, about twenty-five.

"Tired the body, eh," Lino says. Lino is early twenties.

"Yep, take care the body. Eassy eassy," Awai says, but seeing everybody working, he tips back his hat and starts to shovel, "The guy who invented work oughta be shot. Hey, Kyo, what time now?"

I don't have to look at my dollar onion watch, "11:10."

The plantation pays us by gang contract. It's $3 an acre and what the gang makes is divided equally among the seventeen in the gang and everybody has to keep up with Philemon and the pace-setters. On days when we all work hard and fast and make $3 a head, the plantation cuts the rate the next day so that we make $1.50 for the same production. Whenever this happens, everybody says, "See? *Loi loi, buang buang,* you no can beat da plantation," and loafs.

"If it wasn't for my old lady and kids, I get out of here pronto," Awai says.

It's a Filipino gang except for Awai, Mr. Nosawa and me. I can't see why Awai sticks around the plantation, he could go to Honolulu and become a musician or something. Mr. Nosawa is a little younger than father, but he has seven kids all of them young, and he has to make more money than the other Japanese fathers. I'm a little big for my age, five feet seven and 110 pounds and I need to make a little more money than the other eighth graders, and I'd asked to be put with the Filipino cutters and loaders, who do rattooning and *pali pali* and other hard work when it's not harvesting season. They make more money because they're assigned the dirtiest work, and I can keep up with them. They treat me like their kid brother.

Back in the second grade I was run over by a car and had to spend three months out of school. They tried to make me repeat second grade, but I howled. Getting behind a year was like being dropped from earth to another planet. Now I was going to get so far behind I didn't try to think about it. When September came half the guys I graduated with quit their work to go to Pepelau High. My childhood was really over. At least I had lots of company in "Canetop College" in Kahana. At Liliuokalani nearly everybody went to high school. It was better to be in Kahana if you were going to be so poor.

5

One night at supper father talked about a letter he got from grandfather. Grandfather was working for the Canadian ·consul in Tokyo. Father kind of bragged about him, saying that he was educated unlike most of the immigrants to Hawaii. He spoke English so his first job on the plantation was that of a *luna.*

"As far as I'm concerned, grandfather was a thief," Tosh said, spearing a slice of fried potato with his chopsticks.

"Nani!" father's jaw cocked.

Tosh chewed and said, "Grandfather is a *dorobo."*

Father's hand flashed out like a sword.

Tosh pulled back his head. Father jumped at him, Tosh backed off, arms set in a boxing stance. I jumped between them. "Father! Toshio! Stop it!" mother shouted.

"Dog!" father said. "Even a dog knows gratitude!"

Tosh said, "I don't think as much of grandfather as you. Do you want to know why? Because if it wasn't for him, we wouldn't be so poor. We wouldn't be in debt up to our necks. I'd be going to high school and college instead of slaving in the cane fields. He works you and mama for all those years and takes all the money with him to Japan."

"But we gave it to him," mother said.

"He *took* it. You had no choice but to give it to him," Tosh said.

"But father was number one son, and a filial number one son," mother said. "Grandfather cried with gratitude when he left. He said he couldn't ask for more filial children. We did all we could for him. That's filial piety."

"What about piety from the parent to the children? You people are *ko-fuko"* (undutiful to the children), Tosh said.

"Huh!" mother said, "here you work only one year and you talk big. Look at . . ." and she named all the number one sons in Kahana who'd been working for their parents for ten years and more.

"How can you compare me to them? They stupid. They hate school. I like school."

"Don't worry, we won't depend on you. We'll depend on Kiyoshi," mother said.

"Shit. You don't think I'm going to leave Kiyo holding the bag," Tosh said.

Father sat down at his number one spot at the head of the table.

"Sit down and finish your meal," mother said.

"I lost my appetite," Tosh headed for the door. "I still say grandfather is a thief," he said.

Father pretended he didn't hear and in a moment Tosh was gone.

After he left mother said, "Why is he so unfilial? What did we do wrong? Why isn't he like the other number one sons?"

"He's got no discipline. He's like a child, he says the first thing which comes to his mind," father said.

"He's not bad," I said. "He's not a drunk or a gambler like some of the others."

"But he's unfilial, and that's bad," mother said.

"He's not real bad. He's not a braggart or bully or liar like many filial sons," I said.

"But he is bad," mother said.

"Not all bad," I said.

"Kiyoshi, what are you saying? Are you trying to be like him? Your father and I would be heartbroken if we had another son like Toshio. How can you be unfilial and not be all bad?"

"But he's not a woman-chaser or a pool hall bum."

"Still, he's unfilial, and that's bad."

I shut up. I couldn't argue with her.

After a while father said, "The sea was so calm today. There was no current. I could practically see the *papiyos* in the blue water from where I worked."

"That's the story of the past," mother said. "We have to think of the debt from now on, *ne?*"

6

Then it was several months later. We had all bathed and were at the supper table. Tosh was in a good mood. He was training real hard and he felt good. He said, his mouth full of food, "You know I'm real happy there're no Chinese in Kahana."

"Why?" mother said.

"I wouldn't be able to hold up my head to them," Tosh said.

"Why?" mother said again.

"I'd be ashamed to after what the Japanese Army did to Nanking."

"That's a lie," father said.

"It's not only the *haole* papers this time," Tosh said. "I saw it in a newsreel at the Pepelau theatre."

"The newsreel is a lie," father said.

"Boy, you Japanese are really blind!" Tosh said. "It's there in front of your eyes and you say, it's a lie! You just can't see! You don't see what's out there, you only see what's inside your head. Like grandfather. He takes your money, you say you gave it to him. Even when you begged him to leave you enough to live on for a month. You even gave that to him. Black is white and white is black. Inside your head he's like a god. But by his actions, he's a thief."

Father swung at Tosh's head, Tosh slipped and jumped up, father lunged after him, Tosh sidestepped the way he'd practiced with me over and over, and in the same motion threw a left hook to father's solar plexus, as Jimmy DeForest called it, and father crumpled to the floor, holding his belly.

I helped him up.

"Get out! We don't want to see you! There's nobody worse than a child who puts out a hand against his father!" he gasped.

"It wasn't intentional," Tosh said.

"Nemmind!"

Miwa and Hanae and Tsuneko were bawling.

"Get out and stay out! You're a disgrace to the Oyama name!" father stood up and I helped him to his chair.

Tosh sidled toward the doorway.

"Father, you can't let him go yet!" mother said.

"Nemmind!"

"You can't go yet," mother turned to Tosh. "Every child must repay his parents."

"How much? How long? Here I've worked two years and we haven't paid one cent of the debt. We barely surviving," Tosh said.

"Get out!" father said again.

"See what I mean?" Tosh said. "The Japanese are so unrealistic. Take yourself. You can't support your own family. You need my help. But instead of being nice to me, you treat me like dirt. Now you want to kick me out. I'd be glad to go. I can work my way through high school and college and make something of myself."

"Someday you'll have your punishment. You'll have an unfilial son like you," mother said.

"At least I won't saddle him with a $6,000 debt," Tosh said. "And I'll send him to high school and college. You people are upside down. The parents should owe the children, not the children the parents. Look at the *haoles*. Obligation is to the children."

"The *haoles* are inferior. They're wasteful and lazy and extravagant. They treat their parents like strangers, they steal their brothers' wives," father said.

"And they're dirty, they don't bathe every day," mother said.

"They're dirty and inferior, but they don't steal from their children," Tosh said.

"Don't worry, we won't depend on you, we'll depend on Kiyoshi," mother said.

"It'll take him twenty years at least to pay off $6,000," Tosh said.

"Sit down and finish your meal," mother said.

"Shit," Tosh said and walked out.

When Tosh didn't come home by nine, mother sent me to look for him. I headed straight for Citizens' or Single Men's Quarters near the bathhouse. Kahana became a dense dark forest at night. Naked bulbs on lonely telephone poles lit the rutted roads and rain ditches at every intersection. Hibiscus hedges surrounded every yard, and every yard grew ferns, orchids, night flowers, avocado, mango, papaya, soursap, lime, pomegranate, banana, and star fruit. Tall eucalyptus ringed the whole camp and lined the main roads, and there was always a breeze rustling in the night. The stars glittered more brightly than in Pepelau.

There was another thing I'd come to like about the camp. The hundred Japanese families were like one big family. Everybody knew everybody else, everybody was friendly, nobody beat up anybody. I would've gotten into a couple of fights if I were a new student at Pepelau, but the guys in Kahana were open and friendly from the start. They made you feel welcome and invited you to go to the mountains or the ocean. Nobody was left out.

Tosh was sitting on the railing watching several guys shooting crap on the veranda. It was a U-shaped wooden building with a veranda all along the inside. All the single rooms opened onto the veranda. The plantation had a Citizens' Quarters in practically every camp for working sons who didn't get along with their parents. Plantation labor was about fifty percent Filipino and fifty percent Japanese, but practically everybody at Citizens' Quarters was *nisei*.

I sat on the railing next to him.

"Mama been send you?" he whispered.

"Yeah."

"Shit, I so mad, I doan never wanna go back."

I watched the noisy crap game, looking sideways at him every so often. The guy was really getting to be a beautiful counter puncher. He was getting as fast with his hands as with his mouth. I could counter as fast with my left hook, but I could only do it in the ring. I could never hit the old man. I'd think first, and I wouldn't go through with it. But it was a picture book sidestep to the right and a simultaneous left to the solar plexus. There was no pause between the sidestep and the left. Jimmy DeForest would be proud of him, except you never hit your old man, as you never beat up an older brother. He was probably the only number one son in Kahana putting up such a fight, but you couldn't tell because every family was a walled city, and you never knew unless you were inside. And if you were on the inside, you never talked stink about the family, but kept up the family's face.

"I sick and tired getting hit all the time," he muttered. "From now on I goin' dish it out too. You doan know how much he been beat me up when I was a kid. He always called me a crybaby. I was no *samurai*. I had no *gaman* (patience), no *enryo* (holding back). But shit, thass the only way I can fight him. If I start holding back, I play right into his hands. Hard work, patience, holding back, waiting your turn, all that crap, they all fit together to keep you down."

"Maybe you better go live at Citizens' Quarters," I said.

"Shit, you think they let me? It's $5 more for rent."

I sat there for half an hour or so and got up to go home, "You going home?"

"Yeah, shit, might as well."

We went into the pitch-black night.

"Maybe now he'll stop hitting me."

"Why don't you talk to him just plain sometimes. You punch even when you talking. You punch with words," I said.

"Shit, I been try that a hundred times before. They told me to shut up and do what I was told to do. You think papa is tough now, he was real hard those days. You lucky, I been soften him up for you. Thass why you can talk to him. He'd hit you if it wasn't for me. Yeah, I been try. He called me a crybaby, he said I was no *samurai.*"

"But he likes you."

"Sure, he bound to like me. He sucking my blood."

"He's a nice guy, though."

"Sure, he can afford to be nice. He got all the good cards. All he need do is sit tight and do nothing. He not losing nothing. He got no ambition. He's gone as far as he goin' go, so he can sit tight and act like a nice guy. I'm the guy who's losing. They skinning me alive and I supposed to act *samurai* and take it."

"It's not only papa. Every family like that."

"Thass what I mean. The whole system is upside down. You pay and pay and pay and you never pay enough. And they treat me like *I* was the bad guy. They want me to be a nice guy so they can bury me alive. I no can see that. The more you shut up, the better they look. Shit, mama treats papa like he was a *tonosama* (feudal lord). 'It's pitiful for father,' she says. 'We shouldn't bother him, we shouldn't make him feel bad.' Shit, why shouldn't he feel bad when he the one to blame? He the guy on top, he the guy responsible. I no can shut up, I gotta force them to see it my way," he was about talked out when we got home.

"He's ok," I said.

"I wanna hear you say that after you worked twenty years on the plantation for him," he said. "You lucky I been soften him up for you. He used to be real *pakiki.*"

Mother was at her sewing machine in the parlor.

"Where's papa?"

"He's gone to Tsunoda to act as go-between," mother said.

"He's always doing unasked-for favors for others. Why doesn't he help his sons sometimes?" Tosh said.

"Huh, you're not worth his little finger. It's criminal for a son to strike a father."

"You know, it felt good. I didn't feel so angry afterwards."

"It's unthinkable. Unthinkable that it happens in our home!" she said.

"It's unthinkable for him to hit me all the time. That's why I took up boxing long ago."

"You're impossible, you don't even feel bad. Don't worry, we'll depend on Kiyoshi."

"Don't worry, I'll leave after ten years. I'll leave even if the debt is only half paid."

"You'll get your punishment."

"My punishment is now. What did I do to be saddled with a $6,000 debt?"

"You'll be sorry someday."

They argued back and forth. They were both alike. They never let you have the last word and they came out with everything. A guy like father or me had no chance. I went into the bedroom.

Finally Tosh came in slamming the door after him, shouting, "If we were in Japan, you'd probably sell the girls into prostitution to pay up father's debt."

Mother came back with something muffled by the door.

Tosh was steaming again, "Goddam old futts, they still think they in Japan!" he undressed in the dark. He climbed onto the window sill and held open the screen with one hand and pissed into the yard. We all pissed in the spacious back yard at night instead of going to the outhouse, but nobody pissed out of windows as Tosh always did. At least he lifted the screen window.

"That *wahine* she drive me crazy," he got into his bed. "She weak, but inside she nails. She the backbone of the family. But she never let you have the last word."

"You the same way."

"No get smart."

"How come you crab so much?"

"Shit, all I asking for is my body. I doan wanna die on the plantation like these other dumb dodos. Sometimes I get so mad I wanna kill them, you know what I mean?"

"No."

"Papa shouldn't have had more than three kids. Thass all he can support because he got no push. He likes the good times too much."

"It's not all his fault. That's the Japanese and Confucian system. They say, 'A houseful of good children is richer than a warehouseful of goods.' 'A family without children is death to the family line.' "

"Bullshit. These Bulaheads, they no can see they so poor because they poop so many kids. At least mama wants us to be something more than plantation workers, but she wants you to do it after she been squeeze twenty years out of you. Papa, he been do his big thing already, he was a filial number one son, so now he figure his turn to sit back and catch the gravy. I doan think it bother him if we all die on the plantation so long as we filial and give him lotsa face."

That's what the fathers of the Takeshita and Tanaka and Matsumoto boys expect of them, I was going to say, but stopped. He'd stop only if I shut up. He talked so much at times he drove me crazy. I felt like crabbing to the folks too, but he left no room for me. If I went at them after he did, I'd feel like I was piling on. But I really admired the guy. He'd explode and in a flash you'd see something anew, and you were never the same again. *"Kaminari-san"* (Mr. Thunder), Hanae called him.

"All this bullshit about *chonan* (number one son) makes sense only if the old man successful and got property. He leaves everything to the *chonan* and that way he no break up his property. But no father who's a plantation worker can call himself successful," Tosh said.

"Yeah," I lay back in my bed in the dark, hoping he was finished.

It was easy being around father as it was hard being around Tosh. Father didn't disturb anything, and the girls loved him. Maybe he was too easygoing, he loved to talk story and make speeches and act as go-between, and he could sleep anywhere and fall asleep as soon as his head touched the pillow. Mother, Tosh, and I were all bad sleepers and I was the worst. But Tosh was a second father to me since the folks didn't speak English. Whenever I had a hard homework, I had to go to Tosh. Once back at Liliuokalani Mrs. Colon asked everybody to bring a scientific experiment to our fourth grade class. She was skinny and nervous and had broken several yardsticks, whacking the guys who talked during the one-hour sleeping period after lunch. Tosh taught me the experiment of the raw egg in a glass of water. The next day I was the only one with an experiment, "The egg floats," I repeated Tosh's exact words, "because salt contains bouyancy or uplifting force." "You been do it?" Tosh asked me. "Yeah, she been praise me to the sky and called everybody else a dumb dodo." "See what I been tell you? You lucky you follow after me, she know you my brother, she figure you must be smart like me."

He was an "A" student in American school, but about "D minus" in language school. Reverend Kanai, the principal of the Pepelau Methodist Language School, kicked him out of his eighth grade class. Tosh was kept after school for making too much noise. He stood Tosh in the corner while he began the lessons for the ninth grade class. As soon as Reverend Kanai turned around to write something on the blackboard, Tosh climbed out of the window and ran away. When Reverend Kanai turned around to see what everybody was giggling about, Tosh was running off like a rabbit. Father had to go and apologize for Tosh, and Tosh refused to go back to class. He quit going to Sunday School about the same

time, and mother worried he was going to become a juvenile delin-
quent. He pointed to all the Buddhists and non-churchgoers who
were good and all the Methodists who were *chorimbo* types. The
guy was a born black sheep, and sometimes I figured he enjoyed
upsetting you or spoiling your dinner.

But all the fight was over nothing. I'd be fighting in three years.
After a couple of years of amateur, I'd turn pro and make $6,000
in a year. A couple of years later I'd be world featherweight champion, then light and welter, and I'd be making $60,000 a year.

7

In February 1938 Tosh had his first fight in Pepelau. His opponent was Danny Takata, who was washed-up and a drunk. Tosh beat him in three rounds.

"How did I look?" Tosh said.

"Great," I lied. I'd expected more after all the hours working on the Jimmy DeForest course. I thought he'd knock him out in the first round. The second and third fights were the same. He won on decisions, but there were lots of jumping around and jabbing. What happened to all the counters and combinations he'd been practicing? Maybe he was afraid of getting his bridge knocked loose, or his face scarred.

At home Tosh got to be more of a bully with the girls. He went to bed at eight every night, and whenever anybody made a noise he'd yell from the bedroom, "Shut up!"

Six-year-old Hanae had just started first grade. "Huh," she whispered, "how can I get 'A's' in school if I can't study at home." She took her books to their bedroom mumbling, "Don't scold me if I get nothing but 'B's'."

Tosh kept on winning. Each time he fought on the other side of the island and I couldn't go because the plantation didn't supply a truck, he'd come home and wake me up right away and give me a blow-by-blow recap of the fight. "Boy, I been really beat him to the punch! Yeah, he throw one I throw six!" He wanted to take me to all of his fights, but there was just enough room for the five Kahana fighters and the two trainers in the station wagon. But I went to see him every time he fought on this side of the island. It was like I was the one fighting when I watched him. I'd move and duck and bob and weave and jerk my body right and left with his punches, trying to give him English. The guys behind me would watch me instead of the fight. But he didn't look as sharp as when he described the fights on the other side of the island. There were a couple of Kahana fighters, a Portuguese and a *nisei,* lightweight and featherweight, who were KO artists who looked a lot better and who were favored to win the island championships. Nobody really took Tosh seriously. He hadn't fought the two best flyweights, KO Toma from Pepelau and Johnny Yamamoto from the other side of the island. But Tosh kept on winning and made it to the finals which was to be held at Wainae, the county seat forty miles away.

I waited up for him that night. Mother cooked him his favorite fried potatoes and chicken and insisted he eat an orange. She always had an orange or apple. "You have to eat something round so that you can go and return *maruide*" (roundly, without injury). There had been so many flyweights that they were going to fight twice on the night of the finals. Tosh was to fight KO Toma of the Pepelau Athletic Club early in the evening, and the winner of that was to fight the winner of the Johnny Yamamoto–Ken Miyabara fight about ten fights later. They didn't match Yamamoto and Toma for the earlier fight because everybody figured they were the two best and these two knockout punchers would end up fighting for the championship. I'd seen Toma fight and once he hit you with that straight right you were finished. Even if it didn't knock you out, it got you so off-balance and groggy, he'd come right back with it again. But he fought flatfooted and he had to measure before he threw the right.

"How you think I oughta fight him?" Tosh said when he was training for him.

"I don't know. No let him get set. Move around. Jab, I guess." He had me fight like Toma, flatfooted, throwing well-measured rights.

I didn't know how Tosh would do against Toma. He'd looked so unimpressive in the fights I saw him in. He left-jabbed his way to unanimous decisions, but I didn't see how he could do that against a veteran like Toma. Yamamoto, Tosh said, was a swarmer.

Mother, father and I waited up for him. Then past two the station wagon came down "Pig Pen Avenue." We all went out to the lighted veranda. Tosh stepped out. "So long, champ," Mac Fernandez, the trainer said, the door slammed and the car sped away.

"*Katta, katta, tsu taimsu katta!*" (I won, I won, two times I won!) Tosh bounded onto the steps of the veranda and took off his shoes. "Boy! Nobody been give me a chance! I been beat um both, same night! Here they both ten-year veterans! I was real scared with Toma first round, I just jab and clinch and run away, just like we been practice. Second round, I mix it up more, counter more. Third round, the guy's pooped. I hit him every time I want, I can call my shots, I almost knock him out! Yeah! KO Toma!"

"What about Johnny Yamamoto?"

"Johnny, duck soup. His style made-to-order for me. He come in swarming, I sidestep, jab, hook, sidestep, right cross, everything according to DeForest, I tell you I was picture book, I knock him down twice. Auw boy! The reporter from *Hawaii Weekly,* he no even mention me before, he comes to the dressing room and ask me how I learn to fight like that. All the plantation bosses, Keith

Tompkins, all the others they come congratulate me!"

"What about Al Correa and Shige Kawamura?" They were the lightweight and featherweight from Kahana.

"Al lost, close decision. Shige got knocked out. Shige says he hanging up. Shige not in condition. He no train hard enough. Thass why if he no put his man away in two rounds, he in trouble."

Mother sewed a couple of pants for Tosh and he went to Pepelau and bought a sports coat. A trip to Honolulu was a big thing. Only the boxing champs made it, and once in a while when they had a good football team, Pepelau High would go to Honolulu to play McKinley. The Inter-Island Steamship Company made two trips a week from Pepelau Wharf. The Wharf wasn't deep enough so the boats had to wait at sea while the motorboats took the passengers to them. Father packed three cardboard cartons full of avocados to take to our uncle in Honolulu. There were three large avocado trees in our yard. During season they fell to the ground and we fed them to the pigs till the pigs got diarrhea from them. After that we raked them into a pile and burned them when they dried up. Mother had promised me a dime for every one I ate because I was so skinny but I never made a dime.

"That's too many! I can't carry all those!" Tosh said.

"If that's the case, don't go," father said.

"Shit!" Tosh turned to me in English, "He think he sending me on *his* money. He not putting up a cent. I been earn this trip by myself." But he took all three boxes.

Then it was the first night of elimination in Honolulu. We couldn't tell whom Tosh was fighting because the Honolulu papers came to Kahana two days late. But they were broadcasting the fights beginning at nine.

"Is he fighting yet?" mother kept asking.

When the broadcast came on, it was already into the tenth fight. It'd started at 7:30. The announcer gave the results of the previous fights. Midway he said, "And Jose Guildo, five-time territorial flyweight champion TKO'd Toshio Oyama of Hawaii in the second round.

"He's lost already," I said.

"Was he beaten bad?" mother said. Everybody was seated on the parlor floor. I stood up to the bookcase, my ear to the dome-shaped radio.

"No," I said. A TKO was better than a KO. He might have had a cut. Mac might've thrown in the towel.

"He'd better quit," father said.

We all waited for Tosh the night he was to come home. About

8 p.m. a plantation car brought him to the house. He was bedecked with leis and gifts. He gave a lei to each girl and a gift for each of us. He seemed overly happy for somebody who'd been TKO'd.

"Were you hurt?" mother said.

"Nah."

I searched his face. There was no cut.

"How he beat you?"

"Damn Guildo, he play me like a toy. He could've called the second he was gonna put me away."

"He been put you out?"

"Nah, Mac been throw in the towel."

"How many knockdowns."

"Three. You oughta see this guy. He a windmill. You throw one, he throw back ten."

"You better quit," father said.

"No, I got to train harder," he said.

Then he turned to me in English, "Is gonna be hard. Damn these Honolulu guys, they train like pros. They no work, just train."

Tosh worked forty-eight hours a week like everybody else and he worked all day even on the Saturdays he was to fight.

8

After finishing Kahana Grade School in 1938, Takako went to work in the cane fields with the women gang. They did the easy jobs like weeding and planting. In 1939 father and mother decided to send her to Pepelau High School. "Don't educate the girls. They're no good. They'll get married and won't be any help to the family. Educate the boys!" Tosh said, and was told to mind his own business. "She not even good in school!" Tosh said.

Of all the girls, Taka-chan seemed to take care of herself the best. She was one year behind me, and she'd been an average student in both American and Japanese schools. Father had tried to help her by having her write on old newspapers with Japanese brush and ink: *Benkyo wa kofuku no haha nari* (Study and hard work are the mother of prosperity). Father was a good calligrapher, and now in Kahana he was asked to do the calligraphy for all the signs they put up in camp. There was one of his on a one-by-four piece of store paper on the ground floor of the bathhouse where everybody took off his clothes before descending to the bath below. It said: *Shoben bekarazu* (Do not piss). The place still smelled of piss. Mr. Takemoto's calligraphy was refined, almost textbook-like, whereas father's was rugged. But it didn't help Takako. "I can't help it, Kiyoshi took all the brains," she'd say. "You lucky, you know. It could've been the other way, and it'd be real embarrassing for you." In grade school the teachers always put her at the head of the class at the beginning of the year, then gradually demoted her until she ended up in the middle. "Real embarrassing to *me*, you know," she'd laugh. She could always talk back. But Miwa was the other way. She was two years younger than Takako, and Tosh frightened her so much she practically shook each time Tosh shouted at the folks or the girls. She had no comeback and she got to be more and more shy.

At home the fights were getting more bitter. "How much of the debt have we paid up?" Tosh would demand. "I've been working for three years already and nothing's paid up. We're just sending good-for-nothing girls to school. How come you bear nothing but good-for-nothing girls!" "You know," he'd say to me, "if it wasn't for boxing, I think I kill the old futts by now. I get so angry sometimes. All I asking for is my body. I not even asking them to send me to high school. Hell, I can work my way."

He had an intensity and persistence which was scary, and it was getting to be more and more a no-contest. The old man was forty-six, Tosh twenty. The old man acted *samurai*, and Tosh held back nothing. "I look like the aggressor," he'd say to me, "but I not. I fighting for my life. The old man no need be a bully, the system the bully. He can afford to act the nice guy and pretend I doing him wrong. He can afford to be easygoing when he sitting on me and sucking me dry. The other number one sons crab like hell too, but they doan have the nerve to crab to their old men. They crab to me, they crab to each other, they crab to their younger brothers."

Father avoided Tosh, and whenever Tosh said, "Grandfather is a thief" he pretended not to hear. I felt sorry for the old man. He got the message already, and all Tosh was doing was rubbing it in and getting himself more angry and frustrated.

But mother didn't give up, "You'll have your punishment some-day. You'll have a son just like you."

"I hope so. I won't saddle him with a $6,000 debt."

"Debt isn't everything. We could've gotten out of debt if we'd done like other families in Pepelau."

"Who? What?"

"They're rich and put up a big face today, but they were dis-honest and shameful when they were in trouble."

"What did they do?"

"It's too shameful to mention."

"Like stealing? Running away?"

"Lot worse than that."

"Like what?"

"Nemmind."

"See you're doing us another favor. When the family gets into debt, I should be thankful because we're honest. We get into debt because of honesty, not because we're incompetent, not because we're so shortsighted we can't see beyond our noses. Thanks for the honesty, but that was *after* we got into debt."

"Grandfather could've declared bankruptcy and not pay back his debts."

"That's the trouble with the Oyamas. They want to act big and generous and honest with the outsiders. They want to put up a big face at the expense of their children."

"Your father is great. Most sons would be happy to have a father like him."

"They don't know about the $6,000 debt, that's why. They wouldn't touch him if they knew."

"Everybody trusts and respects him. He's self-educated. He knows 5,000 Chinese characters."

"What does knowing Chinese characters have to do with being

able to think ABC to Z? He can't think beyond now."

"You're full of selfishness. You're not a Japanese."

"All I'm asking for is my body. I'm not even asking for a high school education."

"Every child must repay his parents."

"How long? How much?"

They went round and round, neither side giving up. It'd finally end with Tosh walking off, hurling his last insult and getting out of earshot before mother could come back with her last word. Even when we lived in Omiya Camp in Pepelau and mother was sick all the time, she had this fight. The Tanimura brothers and I were gathering algaroba beans every morning before going to school. The pig man who picked up our garbage once a week bought these beans at 10 cents a barley bag for his pigs. Whoever got up earlier picked the kindergarten clean of the long yellow beans which fell during the night. The Tanimura boys got up at 5:30 so mother woke me up at five. They went to 4:30, so mother got me up at four. "We can't have an Oyama lose to anybody," she said, handing me the flashlight and barley bag, and she waited up for me to get back. The Tanimuras finally quit. Now mother was getting physically strong. She wasn't worrying about father's safety at sea or about going further in the hole. Rent, water, and hospital care were free, the plantation even gave you ten gallons of kerosene free every month. Her only worry now was keeping the family together, which meant keeping Tosh and me from running away.

9

In November Tosh started training for the boxing season which would start in February. He trained at home and I sparred with him. In his second year Tosh suddenly blossomed into a picture fighter. He could dance rings around the guys, throw ten punches and get none in return, but he was a counterpuncher and he looked good only if the other guy was the aggressor. He won the island championship again, but he lost on a decision to Phil Pasion in the semifinals in Honolulu. Tosh had beaten Pasion, knocking him down three times, earlier in the year in a dual meet between the Frontier Mill AC and the Japanese-American Club of Honolulu. This time Pasion stayed outside and exchanged jabs and won a close decision, and went on to beat his countryman, Jose Guildo, in the finals. They both made the trip to the National AAU at Treasure Island in San Francisco, and Guildo became the national flyweight champion. A trip to the mainland was like a trip to the moon. Only the territorial champions and the good runners-up made the trip. "Next year," Tosh said.

The plantation promoted Tosh to a truck driver's helper. It was a snap job compared to his former brakeman's job. The several trucks carried the workers to and from the fields, they hauled bags of fertilizer and cane stalks, and they picked up the trash around camp.

The plantation encouraged sports among the workers, and promoted the athletes who were good. There were basketball and football games between camps and then between the plantation champions. Both basketball and barefoot football were classed by weight. There were the 100-, 125-, 145-pound leagues, and barrel weight for those over 145 pounds. Football games were played on Sundays and basketball at night, and the whole camp turned out to watch these games. After Al Correa's and Tosh's good showing, the plantation combined the Kahana and Pepelau Clubs into the Frontier Mill Athletic Club.

Tosh's truck driver was Minoru Tanaka, one of the number one sons mother always praised. Minoru came from a family of eight children, and he'd worked for his parents for fifteen years before he got married. Father too praised him to the skies. At the same time, father would run down somebody like Sadao Kiyonaga, who got married at twenty and left his parents and set up a home of his own. "He's good-for-nothing," he'd say, "he didn't amount to anything."

Minoru was a fat five feet eight. He bossed his younger brothers and sisters, and the younger guys in camp. He always seemed to be scolding somebody. It was only a matter of time before Tosh at five feet five tangled with him. They'd always argued back and forth even while they worked together, and he kept razzing Tosh for getting knocked out by Guildo.

One morning they were picking up the trash around camp when Minoru said, "That Hiromi Izumi, he too ugly, he no can get a wife."

Hiromi was about thirty and he lived five doors above us. He had no neck so that he turned around his whole body when he looked back, but he was a real nice guy. He had a strong radio, which could catch Honolulu direct. I'd go over to his place to listen like when the University of Hawaii played UCLA and Tommy Kalukukui ran back a kickoff for 102 yards. The whole camp knew that Hiromi had been turned down a couple of times. Now father was trying to arrange a match with a girl from the other side of the island. Father was not only president of the Kahana Japanese Club, he'd become a kind of village elder, and wrote letters for people, read their letters when they came from Japan, and acted as go-between.

"What you mean he too ugly? You more ugly!" Tosh said.

"Yeah, but I been get a wife," Minoru said.

"Yeah, they put a blindfold on her, thass why."

"I slap your head."

"Go ahead, go on, slap my head."

"No get smart!"

"You get the nerve saying Hiromi ugly. You ten times more ugly."

"I slap your head!"

Tosh dropped his bamboo rake and stuck out his head in front of Minoru, "Come on, slap my head. Go on, slap my head. I not gonna move till you slap my head."

He straightened up, "See, you yellow. Big but hollow. All mouth."

"I bust you up."

"Okay, bust me up. Come on. I spot you eighty pounds, and I put you away in one round."

"Just like Jose Guildo, eh?"

"You different, you all windbag, big but hollow."

"You better quit boxing, you punchy already."

"You about the ugliest guy I ever met. Nobody in Kahana more fat and ugly than you!"

"I bust you up!"

"Go ahead, go on," Tosh poked his elbow at him. When he backed away, Tosh kept shoving the elbow at him till he nudged Minoru.

"What? You been hit me! You hit me! I not gonna let you forget that! I gonna get even with you someday! You wait! I gonna make you eat spit! I gonna rub your face in spit!" Tosh said.

Tosh went around telling everybody about how Minoru hit him and he was gonna get even with him and make him eat spit.

10

"You shouldn't think of marrying for a long time," mother kept telling me. "Our family is in trouble. Maybe when all the debt is paid, you could go to high school and college. It's senseless to have so many children and not have one finish college. You could become a teacher like Mr. Kuni. And when you marry, marry a nice Japanese girl, don't marry a *gaijin* and turn the family into a chop suey."

All I could think of day and night was girls, but I shook every time I got near a girl. If you got a Kahana girl pregnant, you had to marry her or your family was disgraced. If you started going with her, pretty soon her parents came to see your parents. The only thing to do was to sneak off and see her on the sly. Guys would hide behind hibiscus bushes and meow like cats for the girls to come out. But even then in no time the whole camp knew about it, and everybody waited, it was just a matter of time before the girl got pregnant. Whenever anybody got married, the old ladies would size up the new bride in the bathhouse where she was stark naked and had only a wash rag the size of a hand towel to shield her pregnancy. Slowly everybody in Kahana was becoming related through the marriages.

Kenzo Nishiyama was a kind of a nut. They called him *Taran* which stood for *Taranu* (Not enough), and he was not all there. He was number one son too with a whole lot of brothers and sisters, and he'd work over fifteen years, and his parents had tried to find him a wife without luck. They all found out sooner or later that he was strange. He was a clown and he liked playing with the kids. Whenever he got into talk-fights with the older guys, the guys would always come back with, "Nya, nya, you fock pig, thass why you cleaning pigpen alla time at night. You octopus, you got shit in your head." One night I had two wet dreams and after wiping myself for the second time in the back yard, I got the flashlight and went to our pigpen just below our yard. I just couldn't see it. I had to have a girl. Pigs were too ugly besides being dirty and stinking.

I hated the community bath when I visited *Obaban* and when we first moved to Kahana. It was too large and public, too strange. The three baths, Japanese women, Japanese men, and Filipinos, were housed in a huge warehouse-like building made of corrugated sheet iron. The half dozen Filipino women in Kahana bathed in the Filipino bath before their men came home from work. Each section was separated by corrugated sheet iron, and a large steam plow sat next to the building to heat the water for all the baths. You took off your clothes on the ground floor and went down the long flight of concrete steps into what seemed like a huge concrete hull of a ship. Concrete walls went up fifteen feet to the ground level and high above them were the corrugated sheet iron walls and roof. The bath itself was a small swimming pool. Once I got used to it, I really enjoyed the bath. It was a meeting place, I spent longer than I would in a private bath, soaking and talking.

Another advantage was that it gave me a chance for the first time in my life to see a girl completely naked. The women's bath was built like the men's, and they undressed on the ground level. Late at night when there were no old men around, the guys would peep through a hole. They would pretend they were sitting outside and just talking story, but they would be watching what girls were going in to bathe. As soon as they saw a pretty girl go in, they'd come piling in, fighting for the one hole between the wooden shelves on which everybody kept the family soap and bucket. Most of the girls covered themselves with the small towels. One night I happened to peep, and there was Michie Kutsunai, our neighbor, stark naked! The bulging breasts, the swell of hips, the triangle of hair only a couple of feet from my peeping eye! I almost had a heart attack.

I couldn't get her nakedness out of my mind. I'd sat back to back with her in the toilet while she sang Japanese songs at the top of her voice. I'd sit there and hold back my farts till she left. Her parents were old and her father was extra strict. She couldn't go to any school party or any dance. She and her brother could go only to Japanese movies. I could do rings around her in our eighth grade class at Kahana Grade School, but she was such a brilliant honor student in Mr. Takemoto's Japanese class she made me feel dumb.

I figured nobody would know with Michie. There was a hibiscus hedge and a chicken wire gate between our yards. I didn't even have to meow like a cat. I could catch her in the outhouse. I waited for the next time she came into the toilet at night. She came in one night singing.

"Michie?" I said choking.

"Augh!" she gasped. *"Da re?"* (Who?).

"It's me. Kiyoshi."

"Oh, you scared me."

"Listen, Michie, you junior now, eh?"

"Yes."

"Do you still have your freshman or sophomore English books?"

"What do you mean?"

"Whatever you used for English class."

"Of course. I have a half a dozen of them. We use more than one textbook in high school, unlike the way it was in grade school, especially a hick-town grade school like Kahana," she said in over-enunciated English.

She'd never talked to me like that before, but we'd never talked much.

"You can loan me one?"

"I'd be glad to. Which one?"

She was acting too damn *haolefied*. Whenever anybody spoke goody-good English outside of school, we razzed them, "You think you *haole*, eh?" "Maybe you think you shit ice cream, eh?" "How come you talk through your nose all the time?" Lots of them talked nasally to hide the pidgin accent. At the same time the radio and *haole* newspapers were saying over and over, "Be American. Speak English." Pidgin was foreign. And whenever there was a debate about statehood for Hawaii over the radio, they always came back to the same question, "What about the Japanese and Japanese-Americans? They're foreign, their language and culture are foreign, they can't be assimilated, they can't even speak English after eight years of grade school. What if there's a war with Japan? Whom will the AJA's fight for?" Of the 350,000 people in Hawaii, 150,000 were Japanese.

"Any one," I said.

"Well, that doesn't say anything. Would you like to borrow all of them?"

"Yeah."

"All right, I'll leave them at your home tomorrow."

"Can I get them tonight? I'll wait for you in your back yard." We were talking back to back.

"Why can't you wait till tomorrow?"

"I wanna look at them now."

"Oh, all right." There was a rustle of paper, and she left.

I sat there shaking for a while and went into her back yard.

She came out with an armful of books. "Kiyoshi?" she whispered.

"Here?" I whispered in the pitch black.

"Here," she handed them to me.

In that instant I grabbed for her.

"Aaahhh!" she screamed dropping the books, and ran into the house. I grabbed up the books and ran to our yard. Their kitchen light went on. "What happened?" her mother's voice.

I sat on the swing under the avocado tree and tried to keep from shaking. I couldn't imagine what I was grabbing for. I wanted to grab her and kiss her and I'd grabbed her biceps. I didn't even think. She wasn't pretty and her old man guarded her like a jailer, I thought she'd jump at the chance.

The next time we passed each other going and coming from the bathhouse, she looked straight ahead and pretended not to see me, then said as we passed, "Sex maniac!" I felt like diving into a hole.

I thought of going to the whorehouse on the other side of the island, to which the Filipinos went. But you needed a car, plus $3. I was getting $1.50 allowance a month. Kenji Sueoka had gone there with a bunch of guys, and he came back and bragged to all of us who didn't know what it was like, "Yeah, I been come in two jerk," he bragged. We called him "Two-jerk" after that.

11

Tosh and mother kept going round and round, neither side giving an inch. I took off every time they started. Father too left all the talking and fighting to mother. Maybe because father didn't worry enough, mother overworried, hoping some of her worry would rub off onto you. But Tosh kept coming right back.

One night Tosh said, "Come, les go see Takemoto *sensei.*"

"What for?"

"I wanna ask him about filial piety, if ten years of filial piety is enough. Shit, I been work for three and a half years already, and we been pay back not even one cent of the $6,000. All we doing is surviving. At this rate it'll be over twenty years before we pay it up."

Going to Mr. Takemoto was like going over the immediate boss to the higher boss. Mr. Takemoto was like the father of the whole Japanese Camp in Kahana. He was a tall thin man, whose front teeth kind of stuck out, but he spoke pretty good English and he was a lot less strict than any other language teacher I'd had. But he stressed the same things. The Japanese had this special spirit called *Yamato damashi,* and they had more patience, perseverance, reserve, sense of duty, frugality, filial piety, and industry than any other race. "Be proud you're Japanese," he said over and over. "Don't bring any shame to the Japanese race. Don't shame your family name and your parents. The debt to the parents is deeper than the ocean . . ." In my eighth grade class he'd said, "If your mother and wife were drowning and you could save only one of them, which would you save?" There were five boys and eight girls in the class. "There's no doubt that the white man would save his wife. But what would you do? You have only one mother, you can have only one mother . . ." he'd rub his fingers.

Then he told a story which actually happened in Japan. There was this widowed mother. Her only son and child had a boil near his eye. It nearly killed him to have anybody press the pus out of the boil. She finally cured him by sucking the pus out with her mouth. He grew up boundlessly grateful to her. Then came the Russo-Japanese War and he was drafted. She saw him off to the boat and as the boat pulled away from the wharf, she jumped into the cold water and drowned herself before his very eyes. The son cried. Then he thought about it and got the message. She'd killed herself so that he wouldn't worry about her, so that he could fight well, and sure enough he went to Port Arthur and died a hero's death. "Now, can you imagine anybody but a Japanese doing a thing like that? Do you think a white mother would do such a noble thing?" It was true in a way. You could swing at your mother with all your might as long as you were a boy and under five. After that she started putting the screws on you.

But more than the others Mr. Takemoto stressed honesty, sincerity, trust. He'd illustrate each with a story. When Toyotomi Hideyoshi was a child, he was a houseboy to a lord. During a severe winter he went on an errand which was near his home. After delivering the letter or whatever, he stopped at his home for a bite and to warm his wet feet clad in straw sandals. But his mother wouldn't open the door. "You're in the employ of your lord. Your time is not your own. Come back when you're on your own time."

The worst thing you could be was a crybaby, an upstart who didn't know his place. The noblest person was the man who suffered in silence, not protesting even when he was falsely accused. Another time Hideyoshi was a low-down retainer to his lord. It was his job to guard the lord's straw slippers when the lord visited another lord. This one time it was freezing so Toyotomi decided to warm his lord's slippers instead of letting them just sit on the stone steps. He put them inside his kimono against his chest and held them against his warm body. When the lord came out and stepped into his slippers, he cuffed Hideyoshi, "*Baka!* You've been sitting on my slippers!" Hideyoshi didn't protest. Later the lord found out how Hideyoshi had actually warmed his slippers and how he'd suffered in silence, and he promoted Hideyoshi. Mr. Takemoto didn't explain how the lord found out, or how long Hideyoshi was supposed to suffer in silence if nobody told the lord. But the stories always ended happily.

"Honesty," Mr. Takemoto would say, "is the glue to any society. Without it the best society falls apart. Dishonesty is almost always dishonesty about money. That's why the merchant class is considered the lowest in Japan, below the *samurai,* farmer, and artisan. Without honesty there can be no trust, no sincerity." Maybe it was Kahana which made him talk like that. Everybody was a farmer in a way. The only merchant was the plantation store. Every family was poor with many kids. There was no place to go and you were miles from nowhere.

As we walked to his house next to the language school, I told Tosh about how Mr. Takemoto used to brag about the Japanese spirit.

"Yeah," Tosh said, "the Bulaheads, they good underdogs, but they get the swell head when they get on top."

We sat in the parlor with Mr. and Mrs. Takemoto, while Tosh told them about the family debt. "Father and mother think I should work for them indefinitely. But I don't want to throw away my life. How long must one work to repay one's obligation? I told them I'll work for another six years, and I'll live my own life after that, even if the debt isn't paid. I'll have worked ten years then. Is ten years enough to repay one's debt of gratitude?"

"Hmmm," he rubbed the fingers of his right hand, then left hand, "Hmmm, I guess so. Since this is America and you have a different view of life, hmmm, I guess ten years is about all a parent can ask of a son for the payment of a debt of gratitude."

Tosh practically ran home and he crowed, "Takemoto *sensei* said ten years is plenty! Kiyo was with me, you ask him!"

"Look at Minoru Tanaka, look at . . ." mother came right out with a list of all the number one sons who had been working over ten years.

"Yeah, look at them," Tosh said. "They're all like ghosts. They're dead. They got no ambition left. They all hate it, but they don't have the stomach to fight back."

"It's not courage, it's selfishness. Besides, you talk big of helping us. You haven't been that much of a help. Your boxing expenses eat away half of what you make."

"Like what?"

"Your trips, new clothes for the trips, the time off without pay you take when you take your trips, spending money, special food."

"Tell me, does that cost more than sending Takako to high school? What about her new clothes? What about the $5 a month carfare she has to pay? And here she's not going to pay you back. She'll get married."

12

In November Tosh started training again and I started to train with him. I was 120 pounds and in my sparring with Tosh I discovered I had a natural left hook. I floored him a couple of times even with headgear and 18-ounce gloves. I figured I didn't have to train as hard as he, and from the very first he started giving me advice, "You gonna have to train lot harder than that," he'd say every time I refused to go on roadwork with him.

Then we'd be sparring and he'd say, "You got a girl?"

"No."

"You better not for a while. You get one pregnant, you're finished."

Mother gave me the same advice over and over. Then she'd say, "One boxer in the family is enough. Besides, you're not the boxer type like Toshio. He's like a rooster, he jumps at everything. He's bound to be good in hitting others. You're more composed. You don't enjoy hitting people."

And Tosh never stopped crabbing. In between our rounds he'd sort of pant, mouthpiece in his mouth, "You see the dumb Bula-heads, they like it for their sons to be dumb. They like them to obey. They consider you a better man if you said yes all the time."

"The plantation the same way," I said.

"Yeah, we gotta fight two battles all the time."

In January we started training in the new gym the plantation had built near the basketball court. I worked most on the heavy bag and sparred with Tosh, Correa, a couple of the others. I kept flooring the guys with my left, and my left hook was becoming a legend. "You watch Tosh's kid brother. You think Tosh good, Kiyo is a natural," they said. The plantation promoted me to a truck driver's helper.

I knocked out my first three opponents with my left hook. I'd sucker each guy to throw a right, and when he was recovering his balance, I'd come down with my left, elbow above my shoulder, aiming for the tip of his chin.

"Come on, les go run," Tosh would say.

"Naw, I rather punch the bag."

"You gonna have to work harder than that."

I shrugged. I had my left hook. Besides, I didn't have to reduce the way Tosh did to make the weight. We both made it to the finals at Wainae in March. I was a featherweight and I was to fight a couple of fights after him. I was already taped and in my boxing trunks, but I put on my robe and went outside to watch him. He won easy as expected, but it made me kind of laugh, I'd upstaged him in one short year.

My opponent was Ken Soga, who was stocky and had the build of a lightweight. He could hit with both hands and he didn't back up or stop his boring in and he was always in top condition. I figured I needed just one good shot and he'd slow down or be on the floor. Tosh dressed and came with me and Mac into the ring. "The only way to beat this guy is to jab and keep away. Counter. No try slug it out with him," he said.

The bell rang and I danced into the middle of the ring, and suddenly I found myself in a hurricane, blows coming at me from all over. I kept moving back to get some punching room and he kept crowding and hitting five, six, seven shots to my head, body, arms, neck, temple, everywhere, without my returning one. His blows numbed my arms and ribs and bones and head. I was trying to hold his arms to keep them from punching when the bell rang.

"You gotta keep moving," Mac shouted in the corner.

"My legs shot."

"See, you shoulda gone on all the roadwork," Tosh said. "Fight flat feet, try set him up for a left hook."

The guy didn't slow down in the second round. Up till now I could set my own pace, I could loaf if I got tired, the other guys were scared of me even before I threw a punch. This bastard fought dirty. He fought with condition, not skill. He came at you like a windmill, no style. Damn bastard didn't respect my left hook! I stood flatfooted, tried to block the punches, waiting for the opening. I got in my shot throwing all my 120 pounds into it, wham! right on the tip of his chin, feeling the recoil into my elbow and shoulder. The guy shook it off like it was a tap and slammed a left into my gut. Oh, shit! Go for broke! I started slugging.

The next thing I remember was Tosh slapping my face, "What your name? What your name?" the blinding light over his head. He slapped me again, "What your name?"

"Kiyo," I said to keep him from slapping me more. My head throbbed like the bloated soft belly of a balloon fish. There was a high-pitched ringing pain in the small hard core of my swollen head.

They helped me to the corner and sat me on the stool.

"What happened?"

"He been knock you out clean," Tosh said. "The guy got an iron jaw. Your left hook been bounce off him like a raindrop. You better hang up if you not gonna give it your all. Nobody a natural fighter. You need condition. I would've made mincemeat out of this guy with my Jimmy DeForest. But he'd knock me out too without my legs."

Tosh went on to Honolulu and Phil Pasion beat him on a close decision and went on to become National AAU champ in Boston. "Mac said I had him beat. I thought I been win too," Tosh said. "You gotta knock out these Honolulu guys to beat them." After winning the national championship, Pasion turned pro and Tom Kondo, the manager of Pasion and the Japanese-American AC, wrote Tosh and asked him to come to Honolulu to fight for him. Pasion was turning pro, the letter said, and Tosh could turn pro too anytime, but he wanted both of them in his stable. Tosh could fight as a bantam, Pasion as a fly. "No tell nobody," Tosh showed me the letter.

It meant a cinch trip to the mainland as territorial champ, then fighting for money as lots of the amateurs were doing. They all had a big following in Honolulu, and Tosh was number two to Pasion. Jose Guildo was over thirty and over the hill.

It didn't take Tosh long to make up his mind. On his second day he wrote in his illegible scrawl, he couldn't come now, thanks, because of family obligations, but maybe later. It kind of surprised me. What was the point of all the boxing if you didn't turn pro and make $6,000? The guy was more filial than I thought. I would've gone, but then I didn't really know what it was like to be number one son.

For the next few months I watched Pasion's progress in the *Honolulu Chronicle.* He started as prelim fighter and worked his way up quickly to feature event. They were feeding him setups. But he was drawing a crowd. The other amateurs who'd turned pro weren't as good as he or Tosh. Maybe because there were so many good flyweights in the territory. When you got to be territorial champ, you were as good as national champ. The other weights did nothing at the nationals.

13

It was a long lousy summer. For once in my life I was really mad at somebody. I wanted to kill Ken Soga. But what really got my goat was I'd been so dumb. Tosh was not just one step ahead of me, he was a mile in front. He'd known what it was all about from the very first. All hard work. I started running by myself in the cane fields beginning June. I'd build up my legs and wind. I pushed myself and ran and ran and ran and felt angry at the whole thing. You had to put in ten times the work to get back one part of result. I ran eight miles every day after work, and I got up early on Sunday and ran eight miles. I started feeling crabby like Tosh. Just lots of rice and small slivers of pork or meat with vegetables wasn't enough. *Yamato damashi* (the Japanese spirit) meant you poured your whole being into the single purpose at hand and overcame any physical or material handicap, but it didn't work with me. I needed fish or meat. Bean cake wasn't enough. The Japanese in Kahana had a myth. They were better workers than the *haoles* and Portuguese because they ate rice and the others ate fluffy bread. I began to hate rice. There was too much of it. But I pushed myself and ran and ran, and even as I ran, I kept thinking there had to be an easier way. Boxing wasn't the way. All this work meant maybe I was going to beat Soga, who got beat easy in Honolulu. But for a Japanese there were no jobs except the plantation, unless you went into business for yourself. Even if you went to college, all you could be was a grammar school teacher, and if lucky, a high school teacher. Unless your family had enough money to send you to dental or medical college, and then you came back and practiced in your old hometown. There was no way out but boxing.

I practiced all the parries and sidesteps and counters as Tosh had done, I knew DeForest by heart. Every imaginery opponent I shadowboxed against was Ken Soga. In a year I'd be ready. Then suddenly I got a break. They matched me against Ken at the County Fair on October 12. I started training in the gym when I first learned of it in early September. I asked each sparring partner to come in swarming like Ken, and each time I made mincemeat of him as I jabbed, circled right, sidestepped, countered left hook to belly and face, and came in with a combination as soon as he straightened up. They hardly touched me while I knocked them down. Soga was going to be a cinch.

But the night of the fight I didn't feel well. I'd had a bad sleep, and I felt edgy. When I danced out into the ring, the canvas felt soft and spongy like sand. I couldn't sidestep as quickly, my counters too were a split second too slow; and Ken crowded me giving me little punching room. "What's the matter?" Tosh said after the first round. "I doan know." "You gotta be on your toes. You're fighting flatfooted," Mac Fernandez said.

The next round I kept reminding myself to keep on my toes, and he cornered me less, but it was like I was on a back-pedaling bicycle. He wasn't hitting me as much, but I wasn't hitting him any. "You gotta circle to your right, not straight back!" Tosh yelled between rounds. "What happened to all your counters?" "You're still too gun-shy," Mac said.

I was able to put it all together in the last round. I kept him off with my jab, sidestepped his bull rushes and countered, but I was so tired, my punch was gone.

I felt like hell in the dressing room. I knew I could fight better.

"Maybe you're a gym fighter," Tosh said.

"What's that?"

"Like Jimmy Lee in Honolulu. They say he's ten times better in the gym than in the ring. He leaves his best fights in the gym."

"How come?"

"I doan know. They no can put it all together in the ring."

I kept running and in December Tosh started to train with me. "You gotta lay off every so often, or you go stale." During my long runs through the cane fields, I finally figured out what Tosh had been saying. I'd been fighting myself all along and I was still fighting me. I'd acted overly carefree to hide it and push it down, but now I had to let it out and face it square on and knock it out. It wasn't only me, I was fighting mother and all her overworry which had rubbed off on me, I was fighting Tosh for some breathing room.

The rains started in mid-December and continued to mid-January and I went running on the railroad ties in the cane fields to keep out of the mud. The dead-end U-turn in front of our house became a mudhole, and every car coming down Pig Pen Avenue got stuck. I felt a cold wet gnawing hunger eating away at my stamina, no matter how much rice I ate. I needed more red meat, something which would stick to me. Even my anger was beginning to sound like a whine. Damn Soga. I could beat him if I had the right food to build my stamina on. I began to understand how Tosh felt. Once you got hard on yourself, it was easy to be hard on others. I yelled at my sisters now when they made any noise when I was trying to sleep.

I ran and ran and ran and practiced and practiced all the counters, and I remembered how to breathe once more. Just imagine I was back spearing fish. I'd take a deep breath filling my lungs from the bottom of my stomach to the top of my chest and dive under and stay down for over a minute, then shoot up exhaling everything. I would dive again and again and a couple of hours would fly by like ten minutes. Now I could slow this whirring inside me by pretending I was in the ocean with goggle and spear. You had nothing but your breath to hold on to while you waited and waited for the moment the bell rang. You still jumped the gun, but you didn't make a hundred false starts, you didn't fight a hundred gym fights as before. I didn't try for quick knockouts anymore. I carried each guy to the third round to build up my wind and practice my counters. I beat six guys during the elimination, three by KO's, then met Ken Soga for the island championship.

I felt better at the first bell. I'd slept better. I started dancing right off, jabbing, sidestepping, jabbing, all basics, no fancy stuff. I made him miss and lunge at the air and jabbed him, circling right. I jabbed him silly the second round too. Suddenly it was becoming too easy. I opened up with combination counters in the third, and he stunned me with a combination of his own, and I shifted quickly to my toes, keeping outside, jabbing, dancing out of reach. To hell with being a crowd pleaser. I had to beat him first. I jumped with joy when the bell rang, and Tosh jumped into the ring and hugged me. "Smart fight! You still too easy to hit!"

We both went to the territorial finals in Honolulu. I beat two guys then lost to a guy who didn't even make the semifinals. I still had a long way to go.

Tosh fought Jose Guildo in the semifinals. He floored Jose twice and was far ahead on points when a cut opened up over his right eye in the third round and they stopped the fight. The guy was cursed with the Oyama bad luck. Jose went on to win the territorial title and then the national title in Kansas City. He retired after that, but Phil Pasion was now a main-eventer in Honolulu, and Tosh was still a truck driver's helper. He was called up for the draft and classed 4-F because of a punctured eardrum.

"Well, at least you can thank boxing for that," I said.

"What you mean, boxing? Papa the one. He been hit me when I was a kid."

"You sure?" I couldn't tell when the guy was kidding.

"Sure, I sure. Think about it. Who been beat me bad enough to bust my eardrum? I been KO'd only twice, once from a cut."

"What about the first TKO by Guildo?"

"That was all to my stomach."

"You sure?"

"Sure, I sure."

"But papa never been hit me once."

"You know why he never been hit you? His arm got tired from hitting me, thass why. You lucky you follow after me."

14

In September Miwa enrolled at Pepelau High after working a year in the cane fields, and Tosh blew up again. "Girls are nothing but expense! They're going to get married. They're not going to help the family. It's useless to send them to high school!" "It's none of your business," mother answered back. They argued back and forth like a broken record.

Tosh couldn't see that Miwa's case was special. She'd grown up amidst all his yelling, and now she was scared of her own shadow. She was an average or even less than average student, but she needed high school more than anybody else. She'd end up one of these withdrawn sickly girls. High school graduates married other high school graduates, "Canetop College" people married their own kind, and you couldn't get anywhere on the plantation without a high school education, unless you were an athlete and even then the highest a *nisei* could be was a *luna*.

But Tosh had argued and yelled himself into a hole.

15

Tosh began seeing Fujie Nakama. She was a typical hard-working Japanese girl and she didn't have the fast tongue mother had. She was pretty and she would be perfect for Tosh someday. The only thing was that she was an Okinawan, and the mainland Japanese looked down on them, as they did on practically everybody. Father started saying things like, "The Okinawans cook their party food in the same tubs they boil their dirty clothes." But he never said them before Tosh. Fujie worked as a nurse's aide at the plantation hospital in Pepelau. Tosh would have Takako deliver notes to her when she had a day off and came back to her family in Kahana. She came from a big family too. I'd seen them once together, but even if I didn't, a couple of the guys came up to me, "Hey I see your brother going with Fujie." Nothing was secret in Kahana.

Whenever father spoke, he didn't come right out like mother. He spoke in hints. He'd overpraise the sons and daughters who'd been of great help to their parents, and run down the sons who married young. "That Nakamura Tamotsu, he's no good. He didn't help his parents any. He got married right after high school and started raising his own family." And he knew by heart all the model sons and daughters, "Mitsue Kaneshiro, she's a woman, but she's remarkable. She started working at fourteen, and helped her family till she was thirty-three, sent all her younger brothers and sisters to high school. Not only that, she postponed her marriage another three years to help her family." Then he'd rattle off other names, Minoru Tanaka who's been working fifteen years and was still helping his family, Tadashi Yamada who'd worked thirteen years, Hideo Shimada who worked twelve years, Kenji Watanabe worked twelve years before he got married, Toru Minami eleven years . . . There were many number one sons who were doing this since there were so many large families in Kahana. Tosh always said, "Nothing to do at nights in Kahana, thass why they all poop so many babies."

Tadashi "Crisco" Yamada was my truck driver, and he was one of the model number one sons father and mother held up as somebody I should imitate. He was a tall guy with hunched shoulder and flat round face and crew cut. He was real shy and the guys would kid him, "Hey, you not bad-looking for a Japanese." A couple of years back they'd tried to arrange a marriage between him and a Pepelau girl. He knew the girl, and they liked each other, and the match was almost set when he backed out, saying he wasn't ready. The girl was heartbroken and married somebody else.

"Hey, how come you get cold feet?" the guys kidded him. "I bet you no more what it takes, eh?"

"How come you never been marry Masako Tanoue?" I said one day when we were raking leaves in camp.

He blushed, "I been like her, you know. I really been like her. I wanted to marry her."

"How come you never then?"

"I been thinking and thinking. I got seven brothers and sisters, and my folks still pooping babies, and not all of them right in the head, you know. I been thinking if I get married, nobody around to look after them."

"Who, the old folks?"

"No, my brothers and sisters."

"Kanshin, kanshin" (Admirable, admirable), I said as father or any *issei* would've said.

"No play, you."

There were many guys like him. They had no more push left, they'd been used up.

One night father said at supper, "That Minoru Tanaka is remarkable. He worked fifteen years for his parents before he got married."

"Shit!" Tosh exploded. "Minoru Tanaka is nothing! He won't go higher than a truck driver! He's happy at being a truck driver! He's a bully to his younger brothers and sisters, he tried to bully me, and I told him off! He got scared because he know I can fight! He's so stuck-up, he thinks he's better than anybody. I'm going to rub his face in spit!"

"Why?" mother said.

"Because he hit me. I'm not going to let him forget that! I'm going to make him eat spit!"

"Do you talk like this while working?" mother said.

"He's afraid to say anything. He knows I'm smarter and stronger than he is, he knows I got more ambition than being his helper or even a truck driver! He's nothing but rubbish and you're praising nothing but rubbish!"

Father didn't bring up the subject in front of Tosh again.

16

Then one Sunday I'd gone out early for my run in the cane fields, and came back about ten. Five-year-old Tsuneko came running up as I closed the back yard gate, "Kiyo-chan Wall! Wall!" She was in her bright yellow Sunday School dress and her fine porcelain face was flushed.

I thought somebody in the family had died. "What?"

"Wall!"

"Nani?" (What?) I said in Japanese.

"Senso" (War), she said.

I ran into the house and she came running right behind me as if it was something I could fix. The family was huddled around the radio. "This is no maneuver! This is the real McCoy!" the announcer was saying.

"What's happening?"

"The dumb Bulaheads been bomb Pearl Harbor," Tosh said. He said in Japanese, *"Nihon ga Paru Haba kogeki shita."*

"It must be a mistake," mother said.

"It's real," Tosh said.

"Then it must be somebody else," she said.

"I repeat, this is no maneuver! This is the real McCoy! Sporadic air attack has been made on Oahu . . . The rising sun has been sighted on the wingtips!" the announcer said.

It was like being KO'd. You woke up hot, the skin on your face and hands feeling thicker, callused and barely feeling, you could poke a needle into you and not jump. You've withdrawn inside where it was safer, and left your skin out there in enemy territory, and your mind was regrouping, saying, "It can't be, it just can't be, it must be a dream."

"Nihon wa baka da na?" (Isn't Japan the fool?) mother finally said.

"Sekai dai ichi no baka" (The world's number one fool), Tosh said.

"Are you sure it's not a mistake," mother said.

"Yes, it's not a mistake," Tosh said.

Tosh turned to father, "You have a Japanese flag in the *tansu*. Burn it or bury it. Hide all your Japanese books in the chicken coop. Don't talk in Japanese when there're any non-Japanese around."

Father carried all his books to the chicken coop. He spent most of the afternoon in the shed he'd built next to the coop.

By late afternoon it was a fact. Mr. Nelson, the overseer for

Kahana, came in his big car with several Portuguese and *nisei lunas.* They told everyone to black out his windows. There was going to be work tomorrow, but we had to cover all flashlights and kerosene lamps with blue cellophane paper. There was to be no yellow light. Anyone who disobeyed would be arrested for aiding the enemy. There might be a landing in Pepelau.

"The Japanese are going to kill us," Tsuneko began crying.

"Don't be silly, nobody wants a smelly place like Kahana," mother said.

"Where's father?" Tosh said when he didn't show up for a couple of hours.

"He's in the chicken coop," mother said.

"He's not there," Takako said. "I just went there."

"Crazy old man," Tosh said in English. "He's still trying to act the old village elder."

"Where did you go?" Tosh said when he showed up an hour later.

"There was some unfinished business with the Japanese Club," he said.

"The Japanese Club is *pau* already, you understand?" Tosh said. Father nodded.

It just didn't make sense, I kept thinking. Here they worried you to death, made you a nervous wreck, don't do this, don't do that, don't do anything that'd bring shame to the Japanese race, don't be a rotten apple and spoil the whole barrel. What chance have I got, me, a single apple getting slammed by a barrelful of rottenness? Even if I tried deliberately, every day of my life, I wouldn't be able to produce one-thousandth of the massive shame of Pearl Harbor.

When night fell it was like anything could bust out at any minute. They might land any time any minute. A warning was passed from house to house in Japanese Camp. The Filipinos were mad and they might attack any Japanese. Nobody should go into Filipino Camp, nobody should work with them by himself in the cane fields. It was extra dark when we reported to the office at five next morning. All the headlights of the trucks were covered with blue cellophane. I worked with a blue flashlight. "Crisco" and I were assigned to truck Mr. Soniega's Filipino gang to their field. The *luna* rode in the cab of the truck with the driver, and I rode in the back with the workers. I was going to be alone with all seventeen of them, but hell, I'd work with them for four years. "Hi Lino, hi Philemon," I said as I always did, and they said "Hi Kiyo," but there was no laughing, no horseplay. Everything felt subdued like anything could still bust out.

The week passed. The Japanese didn't land. All the ROTC students at the University of Hawaii, McKinley and Farrington were called out to form the Hawaii Territorial Guard on the first day, and there were many *niseis* among them. At the same time the *niseis* who'd been drafted in the Army were kicked out of their outfit and assigned to do labor work like stringing barbed wire at beaches. Their guns were taken from them. There were all kinds of rumors. One of the Japanese pilots shot down wore a McKinley High School ring. Patches had been cut in the cane fields in the shapes of arrows, all pointing to Pearl Harbor. The FBI came up to Kahana and grabbed Mr. Hamaguchi. He'd been doing some part-time work for the Japanese consulate. There was a consulate representative like him in every camp and town; father had acted as representative in Pepelau. He reported births and deaths of Japanese and put in applications for canceling Japanese citizenship. A few days later, Mr. Baldwin, the manager of Frontier Mill, kicked out the whole Hamaguchi family from Kahana. It was plantation policy to kick out families without males of working age. All the Buddhist priests and the teachers in the Buddhist language schools in Pepelau were taken away. The president of the Japanese Club of Pepelau was grabbed. It was only a matter of time before they came to get Mr. Takemoto and father.

17

I had to talk to Mr. Takemoto before they grabbed him. The guy was unusual for an *issei*. His wife was weak and he had only two kids, but I doubt if he'd have had more even if she were strong, if he couldn't support them. The families in camp chipped in so much a month for his salary. Most *issei* had this *pakiki* mind, they got an idea and that was it, all the facts in the world couldn't make them change it, and they got mad if you contradicted them or brought up a subject which shouldn't be brought up. Even father was like that on one subject. He'd been kidding mother about being such a worrywart back in Pepelau, and I'd said jokingly, "You ought to divorce him." He nearly jumped a foot in the air, "That's no joke! Divorce is nothing to joke about!" It was the closest he'd come to hitting me. Divorce was a forbidden subject, a dread disease which only the *haoles* had.

You could ask Mr. Takemoto anything and he never blew up, and he wasn't like Mr. Kuni and the other *nisei* teachers, who dodged your questions and made fun of you. I'd asked Mr. Takemoto once, "The *haole* papers keep saying the Japanese can't be assimilated because they don't intermarry. Shouldn't the Japanese intermarry more?" Another time in our one-hour-a-week *Shushin* (Morals) class I'd said, "Shouldn't the *nisei* fight for America in case of war with Japan?" He rubbed his fingers, "Hmmm. Yes. It's like a wedding, where the bride cuts off all relationship with her original parents and is reborn a member of her husband's family. That's why she wears a white death robe beneath her wedding kimono. It's a symbolic death and she can't go back to her old family. In this case it's as if the *nisei* is the bride and America the groom."

I went to his house one dusk after work. The language school was boarded up and he was out of a job. I'd pushed all the unpleasant things to the back of my mind. I'll think of them later, I said, unlike Tosh who caught everything on the first bounce.

I sat on the couch in the parlor and faced him, "*Sensei,* the Japanese make such a big thing about honesty and trust and sincerity. You keep saying, '*Nihonjin no kuse ni*' (How can you be a Japanese and do such a thing?). When we used to play *samurai,* we would shout like they did in the movies, '*Sa koi, ichi do ni kakkate koi!*' (Come, come all at once!) You used to tell us stories of Yoshitsune and the others. They rode out by themselves in front of the enemy and shouted their names and ranks and challenged others of equal rank to come out and fight. '*Bushi ni wa nigon nashi'* (A *samurai* never goes back on his word, he's not two-faced, he doesn't need a second word), you used to say over and over. None of us came from *samurai* families, but you and everybody else expected *samurai* behavior out of us. So how can you explain Nomura and Kurisu? How can you be a *samurai* and still attack Pearl Harbor without declaring war?"

"Hmmm . . . I can't say. I don't know what happened. It's different when nations and nations fight, it's not the same as individuals fighting individuals. I don't know what went on."

"But isn't dishonesty dishonesty? And isn't dishonesty shameful?"

"Yes."

"So how could the Japanese act like that?"

"Maybe because in modern war, there are no rules. The Japanese began the Russo-Japanese War by a surprise attack on Port Arthur. But the Russians goaded them into war, and the whole world praised the attack as courageous."

"Did America goad Japan to attack Pearl Harbor?"

"I can't say."

"But if somebody goaded you into a fight, would you sneak up on him and hit him from the back?"

"No."

"Then why would Japan?"

"It's hard to say, but you can't judge nations as if they were individuals. Nations act on a pragmatic basis, they do what they think is best for the moment. They'd do things which all the factions can agree upon."

"You know, you've always said, 'Be proud you're Japanese.' 'Never bring shame to the Japanese race.' What if they, all of them, bring shame to me? What about me? I feel ashamed I'm Japanese. I feel a shame I can never erase, and here I haven't done a single bad thing."

"Yes . . ." he rubbed his fingers, "it's hard to explain things rationally."

"But if you thought something out before you did it, you could at least explain to others why you did it."

"The Japanese don't think rationally. They act pragmatically, they do what is best for the moment."

"They'll be making the same mistake over and over then."

"It's something else they have. *Shimakuni konjo*" (The narrowness of an island nation).

I sat there watching him rub his fingers. I felt silly being angry at him.

"Is there any other explanation?" I said finally.

"It's so hard to find explanations. Japan is such a poor country, she would starve without outside resources."

"So she steals from others in the name of survival."

"The British, French, Dutch, Germans and others did the same thing a hundred years ago, not for survival but profit."

"But Japan is a hundred years behind the times."

"Yes, that's it, maybe. Japan isolated herself for 250 years between 1600 and 1860 when other nations were becoming nations and getting used to dealing with each other as nations. So Japan grew up into a nation without that childhood period . . . She was going in the right direction till in the 1930's when the military assassinated all the moderate leaders and took over the government."

"But all the people are behind the military now."

"It's hard not to be behind your government in a war. The only alternative to a war many times is civil war."

"But isn't that better? At least you're not harming outsiders for your family differences."

I sat there unwilling to leave. The tea which Mrs. Takemoto had brought out was now cold. But I'd come hoping he'd tell me something which would make me feel better. Nothing I do, nothing in my future life will make me feel so low. I'd been knocked out so badly I'd never recover, there'd forever be a ringing in my head.

"You know," I said, "the Japanese make such a big thing of *Yamato damashi*. Actually it's a very dangerous thing if it goes in the wrong direction, isn't it? It has no restraint, and in the wrong direction it becomes another Pearl Harbor, another rape of Nanking."

It was a blacked-out night I walked out into when I finally said, "Good night." The once proud ground I'd been standing on had turned into soft shit, and I became a zombie. I'd stare at mother and father for long periods, I'd walk and walk in the night. I felt a flutter of pride when they sank the Prince of Wales and Repulse. At least they can fight without a sneak attack. But it wasn't a racial war, they were like a disease, and the sooner they were beaten the better. It was like watching your older brother whom you'd believed in and loved now running wild committing murders. Maybe I was becoming too much of a moral worrywart, judging like I was perfect. What if grandfather had been successful and had sent for father and mother? We'd have been too young not to go. We'd have grown up in Japan, and where would I be? Would I feel the way I do now? Would Tosh be able to put up his kind of a fight if he were fighting the whole country besides the old man? It was not only "lucky come Hawaii," but "lucky *stay* Hawaii." War was war. But it wasn't as simple as that. Everything, even wars, had certain basic rules.

The more I brooded, the more I felt like a crybaby. After a while everything began and ended with me-me-me and my mental comfort. After a while I was asking: How could they do this to me? Thank God, Tosh was the way he was. He didn't brood or stare askance at his parents or go walking in the night. The guy was so external. He said at the supper table, "Japan would be lucky to lose to America, that is, if they don't all commit suicide before they surrender. America is not petty and harsh like Japan. America would overthrow Japan's generals and give the government back to the civilians."

Father and mother nodded. They whispered a lot between themselves now, wondering about what was happening to relatives in Tokyo and Wakayama.

Mr. Yoei Sato had been a private in the Japanese Army. He went around saying Japan was going to win. He was a *hanawai* man like father, but when the Japanese took over he was going to be in charge, he said, because he was the only ex-Army man in Kahana. He was so *pakiki* he'd be a chicken-shit dictator if he were in charge.

The second week went by and they didn't come to get father and Mr. Takemoto. We learned that it was because Reverend Sherman had gone to the Army and sworn over and over that everybody in his church was loyal to America.

18

On the third Sunday after Pearl Harbor a brand-new car stopped in front of our house. Out stepped a *haole* with a crew cut in an aloha shirt. He wasn't one of the plantation *haoles,* and he strode like he was all business. A *nisei* or *kibei* in khaki uniform trailed alongside.

"I would like to talk to Mr. Oyama alone," he said and the *kibei* translated.

Tosh, mother, myself and the four girls waited in the back yard among the mango, avocado, papaya trees and the rows of bananas father had planted.

"What if he's pulled in?" Tosh said to mother.

"Can't be helped," mother said. Tsuneko was whimpering.

"Papa's lucky he became a Christian."

"Yes," mother said.

We waited and waited. It was like we were always waiting for him. The days and nights he'd spend at sea. Those who were taken away just disappeared, nobody knew where they were taken to.

Suddenly after an hour father came paddling in his clogs looking for us, *"Oi"* (Hey). The young FBI man was behind smiling.

"Okay, papa-san, mama-san," the FBI man said.

"Ocha ikaga?" mother said. "How about some tea?" the soldier translated.

"No thanks," the sandy-haired *haole* said. "We have to be going," he said.

"The first thing he asked about was the $7,000," father said.

"What $7,000?" everybody said.

Father had taken a day off in November on some business in Pepelau, but we didn't ask him why or think anything of it. Some Japanese Club business. He'd read in the bilingual paper that all the bank accounts of Japanese aliens and organizations were to be frozen within a week, so he'd gone to the Bank of Hawaii in Pepelau and withdrawn the $7,000 deposited there in the name of the Kahana Japanese Club. He brought it home and hid it in the shed beside the chicken coop. He'd approached the couple of *nisei* members of the club, and asked them if they would have it redeposited under their names. One of them said he would, but he could never get a day off to get to Pepelau. On December 7 the $7,000 was still in the chicken coop shed, and father went to each member's house in Kahana and gave him his share after he had deducted $500 which he explained they would contribute to the Red Cross. It amounted to over $70 for the ninety-odd members.

"I would do it all over again," father said to the FBI man. "The $7,000 represented the dues the members had paid over the years. It was money earned from working in the cane fields for less than a dollar a day in the early days. It belonged to them. The paper said it was going to be frozen, so I went to get it. Why didn't they stop me then if it was illegal?" and he showed the FBI man the receipt from the Red Cross for the $500 contribution.

Then the man asked through the interpreter, "Whom do you want to win?"

"Neither side. I want Japan and America to be friends," father said.

"If the Japanese invaded Kahana, would you shoot them?"

"Yes, if he's the enemy. If he's going to shoot, I'd shoot first."

"What if he's your cousin?"

"How can you tell if he's your cousin at that distance? I'd shoot."

"Are your sons dual citizens?"

"No, I canceled their Japanese citizenship," he got the papers from the bedroom.

"Okay, papa-san," he laughed.

"The crazy old man," Tosh said to me that night in the bedroom, "he lucky nobody been steal the seven g's. We'd be thirteen g's in the hole. Shit, I wish he look after his own family like that. The guy loves to make speeches and act the big shot." But he wasn't ranting anymore. The anger and bitterness were gone. The debt had been pushed into the background the way a toothache is dwarfed by a brain hemorrhage.

19

The next few months crawled by. Hawaii was under martial law. Everybody was frozen to his job. A Japanese was forbidden to carry more than $200, and no more than three Japanese could congregate at one place. The *niseis* in the Hawaii Territorial Guard were discharged as untrustworthy. All the Japanese on the West Coast were pulled in, and it was only a matter of time before they came to get us. They were going to send us all to Molokai.

School resumed in January, and Tsuneko who was in the first grade would tell me of the latest happening. They got into talk-fights with the Filipinos and Portuguese, who called them "Japs" and *"daikon* farts." But she wasn't scared because the Japanese outnumbered them. Mrs. Boyle, the principal's wife and first- and second-grade teacher, ran from the classroom into the shelter in the schoolyard, screaming, "The Japs! The Japs!" when an airplane flew unusually low over Kahana. She hid in the hole and had her pupils cover her with the palm fronds they used as camouflage. Mrs. Boyle had her dresses made by Mrs. Ansai on Pig Pen Avenue, but now she didn't dare come into Japanese Camp. She sent one of the older students to get her dress. The people of Japanese Camp laughed about it, but they themselves were afraid to go into Filipino Camp.

Mr. Watada who was half-Japanese and half-Hawaiian and married to a full Hawaiian, changed his name to his mother's Hawaiian name, Kalani. His two grown sons kept their Japanese names, however. There were many *haole* soldiers from the states now in Pepelau and many Japanese girls started going with them. None of the Kahana girls did, but every mother warned them about going out with *haoles.* The *nisei* started calling themselves AJA's, Americans of Japanese ancestry, *nisei* was too Japanese.

Then gradually things started to change. The pre-War *nisei* draftees were formed into the Hawaiian Provisional Infantry Battalion and sent to Wisconsin for training. They were going to be allowed to fight in Europe. Father's luck too seemed to be changing. Had he stayed in Pepelau, he would have been pulled in as consular representative. If he wasn't, he'd be out of a job. All the Japanese fishermen, which was ninety-five percent of the fishermen in Pepelau, were forbidden to go to sea. Reverend Sherman talked Mr. Baldwin, the manager of Frontier Mill, into giving Mr. Takemoto a *hanawai* job in the fields.

In June 1942 Tosh asked father and mother if he could marry Fujie Nakama. I thought there was going to be another explosion, but surprisingly the folks said okay. They must've figured he'd go ahead and do it even if they said no. They made a lot of noise before it happened, but once you did it or let them know you were going to do it anyway, they backed you up. It was the other way around now. They would suffer more if they cut you off. Even mother held her tongue and didn't bring up all the filial number one sons. It surprised me that Tosh wanted to get married so young. He was twenty-two and he'd been working for the folks now for six years. Tosh said he'd give the folks one-third of his pay, and all of Fujie's paycheck for a year. After a year, he'd give them only his one-third.

It was a small sad wedding. Reverend Sherman asked the Army to relax the no-more-than-three-Japanese rule, and he came to the house to marry Tosh and Fujie. I'd never thought much of Reverend Sherman before the War. He was like another nice-guy *haole* teacher, except Snooky; he was like another nice-guy *nisei* teacher. But now Reverend Sherman showed a lot of guts and he went out of his way to fight for you.

Tosh and Fujie moved to a plantation house in Pepelau. Tosh's new job was hauling bagasse from the mill in a ten-ton truck. He worked from 6 p.m. to 6 a.m., and he began a correspondence course in engineering with a school in Chicago, and he studied his algebra and geometry during the long hours he waited for his truck to fill up with bagasse. "Gotta get out of this plantation," he kept saying. But I could see Tosh simmering down visibly. Fujie was good for him.

As long as Tosh was home, I kept wishing he'd stop crabbing so much. But now I missed his crabbing. I couldn't crab the way he could, and things kept building up in me. All this reserve and discipline and patience and self-sacrifice only wore you down and made you feel real low.

I couldn't shrug off the six g's anymore. Boxing was out. It was going to take ten more years at least, and here I was frozen on the plantation at $2 a day. It was like a prison term. It was going to drain ten years of my life, six days a week, eight hours a day, and at the end of it, there'd be nothing to show for it.

I tried to find all kinds of excuses for father. He was too good-natured and trusting. He wouldn't even check the weights of his catches. He'd sit in the back room drinking and talking story with Mr. Chatani while Mrs. Chatani weighed the large baskets of fish and told him the figures. He wasn't a good businessman. He'd take me and my friends for a day of fishing on his boat, give up a whole day of gas, bait, and ice just to give us a treat. Then he'd take us out again even if we all got seasick the first time and begged him to take us home.

One Sunday afternoon father was working in the chicken coop, and I went for him, "Father, how did you get into such a big debt?"

He stopped, startled, "Hmmm. The Depression. All the fish in the area had been fished out. There were too many fishermen."

"Why didn't you quit earlier? Before your debt became so large?"

"It happened so suddenly. You remember when mother had all her teeth pulled and collapsed. I stayed home for three months looking after the children. For three months there was nothing but expenses with nothing coming in."

"It all happened in three months?"

"No, the three months were the worst."

"But you don't go $6,000 in debt in three months."

"No, it happened long ago. I never really got out of debt since leaving the plantation. I had to buy a boat. And fishing is gambling. You could put in twelve hours a day and lose money. You don't catch enough to pay for the gas and bait and ice."

"Why didn't you quit earlier then?"

"I couldn't. You've seen how miserable plantation work is. We used to do the same work, and get paid less than the Chinese and Portuguese."

"But what about me and Toshio? We don't have a chance. We'll be old men by the time we pay off the debt."

He sighed and looked away, *"Oya ga ko wo shippai saseta kana?"* (Has the parent made the child fail?).

I took his hand and shook it and kind of patted his shoulder, "Our luck will change."

I felt sorry for him. It wasn't all his fault, grandfather had got him into debt and once you went in the hole it was hard to get out. Father wasn't as haughty as Tosh said. It was the Japanese way, face was that much more important, like the starving *samurai* who walks around with a toothpick in his mouth, pretending he'd just eaten. You covered up more, and it was rough when you were the one being covered up or you were holding up somebody else's face. But everybody did it. Like the family with a kid who was not all there. He was kept hidden or treated like there was nothing wrong, and no matter how much he was loved by the family, the kid knew he was a black eye on the face of the family and the poor kid never recovered, never had a chance. Face was pretending to be perfect or there was nothing wrong, and either way the losing of face meant exposure and shame. You ended up pretending and hiding too much, you ended up with all kinds of skeletons which shouldn't have been skeletons in any closet. You ended up covering for those above you, even defending their wrongs as right. It was too much. Many fathers were miniature emperors, they took everything for granted, they didn't even say "Thank you." But father was different. He could and did change, and he never crowded me like Tosh or mother, not openly anyway. He always treated me special, maybe because of the car running over me in the second grade. Even before then. When I was five I spilled a can of paint on the deck of his sampan he'd brought ashore to paint. When he found me a couple of hours later hiding under the boat, he said, "You should tell me right away next time. Paint is hard to clean when it dries." Then when Biggie Don beat me up when I was in the fourth grade, father shot off like a cannon ball to Baldwin Park and beat up Biggie. And he was a hard worker. He'd spend many Sundays and many hours after work planting a new banana patch, new papaya trees, building a new chicken coop. Just his luck was bad.

20

Tosh had buried the hatchet after Pearl Harbor. He was top man in the family now. Father and mother who spoke no English depended on him and me to stay out of trouble, and he was a good winner. All the talk about rubbing their faces in spit had been only talk. But suddenly the debt became a raging toothache again.

He screeched his big Mack truck to a stop on the road beside Citizens' Quarters, "Kiyo! Hey, Kiyo!"

I jumped over the veranda railing and ran, thinking something awful had happened.

"You know mama is five-month pregnant?" he nearly exploded, sitting in the cab of the truck.

"No."

"And Miwa pregnant too!"

"Who?"

"Hachiro Shiotsugu!"

He was a senior at Pepelau High.

"How you know?"

"My wife works at the hospital!"

"How long she pregnant?"

"Three months! Not only that! My wife expecting! She two months along!"

"You sure about mama?"

"Yeah! I just talked to them. They ashamed to let us know. Goddam old man, he no can see beyond his nose. He makes seven children, and that's it, all *pau*. He no think about who's gonna support them. He no can look ahead. He no can afford more than three kids, and here he gonna get his seventh! I so mad, I wanna kill them!"

Tosh went to Hachiro's older brother and told him, "You guys think you marrying into a good family, but you not. Our family look good from the outside, but we six g's in the hole. Thass why we moved back to Kahana. The old man is all face, we the poorest family in Kahana."

The wedding was small and even sadder than Tosh's. Hachiro would finish out his year in high school, then go to work in the cane fields. Miwa, a sophomore, quit, and they lived with his parents and five unmarried brothers and sisters.

Tosh turned into a madman. Every time his work took him near Kahana, he'd drive the big truck to the end of Pig Pen Avenue, "I told you, and I told papa, don't send the girls to high school. They'll be nothing but expense! They'll get married!"

"Shikata ga nai" (It can't be helped), mother said.

"Shikata ga aru! You people can't see beyond your noses!"

Mother would cry and after he left, Hanae and Tsuneko who'd been hiding in the bedroom would come out and comfort mother. Six-year-old Tsuneko acted as messenger. Whenever she saw Tosh's truck coming into the camp, she'd run with all her might to the house, *"Oni ga kita! Oni ga kita!"* (The ogre has come!). She'd hide in the bedroom and wait till he left. When Miwa already big with child was at the house, she'd run into the cane field like she was being chased by a ghost. She'd stay there till Tsuneko went out to get her.

"You said every child must earn his keep! How come Miwa isn't earning her keep!" Tosh said.

Mother said, "It can't be helped. It's like raising pigs. There's bound to be wastage."

"So we're pigs now! Oyama's pigs! Why didn't you stick to raising pigs!"

"Don't worry, we won't depend on you. We'll depend on Kiyoshi."

"You're going to kill him. He'll be an old man. Someday he's going to get mad and kill you!"

"He's filial, unlike you."

"My child isn't even going to have grandparents. He'll have an uncle or aunt three months older than him, and a nephew or niece one month older. How come you raise more pigs than you can support! All good-for-nothing girl pigs! I bet if this was Japan, you and papa would sell the girl pigs into prostitution and think nothing of it! You'd call it filial piety! It's filial bullshit! I told you and papa over and over. Educate the boys, not the girls! You're going to depend on the boys later! And every time you told me to shut up, it's none of my business! As soon as the debt is paid, I'm going to disown you and papa! I'm cutting you off for good! I'd have been happier as an orphan than having you as parents! You raise us like we were pigs! Oyama's pigs!" he stalked out, leaving mother in tears.

Tsuneko came crawling out of the bedroom on all fours, saying, "Oink, oink, oink . . ."

Mother went from tears to laughter.

Tosh kept coming back, yelling louder each time. Father avoided him. It was mother who had to absorb the brunt of his anger. But it was senseless. Nothing more was being said, only more hurt, more salt rubbed into the wound, but he couldn't keep away. Mother's only argument finally was, "We won't depend on you, we'll depend on Kiyoshi," and Tosh's counter was, "You think I can leave Kiyo all alone? You'll take advantage of him and milk him till he's an old man!"

When mother went to the plantation hospital, Tosh refused to go see her. Fujie worked there and saw her every day. It was a boy and father named him *Jyun* (Gentle). At least the old man's luck was changing. I caught a ride on Sunday and went to see her.

"Aren't you ashamed to have an old mother like me give birth?"

"No, I'm glad I have another brother."

"Toshio refused to come to see me."

"I know. Probably he's jealous for his unborn child. You'll love Jyun more."

"I can't help it. He's my own child."

"I know."

"Someday when you get married, you should learn how the *haoles* do it."

"What?"

"How they have so few children. You shouldn't have more than three children. It's too hard."

It kind of surprised me. First I'd thought she was too old to have children. Now she knew nothing of rubbers, when I knew of them when I was in the third grade. We'd find the used ones, all stinking and rotten at the beach or at the school yard, and one of the older guys would hold it up at the end of a stick and explain what had happened. But the only place that sold them was the drugstore in Pepelau.

"Why did you call him Jyun?"

She laughed. "I asked father not to give him any fierce-sounding name. When you and Toshio were born, father gave you both such strong names that I got sick. I didn't want to get sick again."

"How do you feel?"

"Fine. How are Tsune-chan and Hanae and Miwa and Taka-chan?"

"Fine."

One thing father could brag about. He had seven children and there was nothing wrong with any of them.

21

I was making only $50 a month as a truck driver's helper, and turning over $45 for the folks. The guys who left for the high-paying defense jobs in Honolulu got arrested. I began to feel more and more like "Crisco." I'd visit him at the Citizens' Quarters, thinking, there's me ten years from now. There was a crap game there every Sunday afternoon, and I'd sit on the railing and watch them play on a blanket on the veranda floor. Hiroshi Sakai, who was my classmate at Liliuokalani in Pepelau, always showed up for the games. His father was a cab driver and he was a cab driver, but it was only a front and he showed up wherever there was a game. Hiroshi was a terrific pool player and gambler. It was weird the way he kept winning. Whenever he rolled, the dice rolled in unison like the wheels of a cart, and even when one die rolled ahead of the other, neither flipped on its side. The Kahana players finally refused to fade him, and he stopped coming.

I kept going to Citizens' Quarters every night and Sunday just to sit there with "Crisco" and the others. We didn't talk much about what was bothering us, there was no point, we were all in the same boat. The Quarters were the farthest we could run away to. The War was going to last forever and martial law froze us to our jobs forever. Everything was exploding in the rest of the world while we were like some prehistoric monster frozen in ice.

The rain started in the middle of December and didn't stop. The roads got so muddy my wooden clogs would get stuck in the mud and I'd lose them several times in my three-block walk up to the bathhouse or Citizens' Quarters. Everybody wore a sweat-shirt over his aloha shirt and carried a bamboo-ribbed oil paper umbrella.

I had the bedroom all to myself now that Tosh was gone, and at night the room turned into a kind of snug cave with the wind and rain at the window pane. I couldn't sleep nights for thinking of Sachiko. Mr. Nosawa had been inviting me for supper once every three months or so ever since we both worked in the Filipino gang back in 1937. Sachiko, who was twelve then, had waited on me like I was the man of the house. She'd jump up and insist on refilling my half-empty bowl of rice; she'd keep my teacup filled; she'd put out a new helping of fish or meat on my plate. She was the oldest child of the family, and I looked after her like an older brother. She went to work in the fields after finishing grade school, and whenever "Crisco" and I went to pick up the gang she worked with, I'd go into the fields and help her instead of waiting on the truck. The old women of the gang would tease her or me, but I shrugged it off, we were practically brother and sister.

Suddenly she was a breathtaking seventeen, the face of a rare orchid, the body of a ripe lush mango. She'd been giving me signals all along without my taking them seriously. She'd lean a breast into my shoulder when she refilled my teacup. Another time we were all alone in her yard and she stumbled and fell into my arms. I'd bump into her continually during my roadwork before the War. I'd always stop and help her with the pig grass she was cutting and stuffing into barley bags. She was just like a kid sister. But now every time I turned around, there she was, naked, spreading her arms and legs. She came out of the walls at night and drove me crazy. The closest I'd been to a girl was at the Kahana Young People's Association's New Year's Eve dance. I couldn't dance. I'd shuffle back and forth, legs quivering, palm sweating, hoping the music would catch up with me and turn me into a dancer. It'd worked in surfing. The swell had swept me and my washboard before it and turned me into a surfer. But it didn't work on the dance floor. The music never caught up with me, I was too conscious of the closeness of the girl, of how awkward a hard-on would be. All this discipline was like pinching a balloon, I bulged somewhere else, especially inside my head.

I couldn't sleep many nights and I'd give up. I'd give up everything, renounce the world outside the plantation, provided I could have Sachan for myself in a plantation house all to ourselves. We'd spend the rest of our lives in the rapture of each other's arms and body. I would ask for nothing more than to imprison her within four walls and imprison myself with her in a lifetime of lovemaking. Tomorrow I'll go get her and we'll run hand-in-hand into the nearest cane field and not come out until we've loved and loved and explored the magic of our bodies.

But when I got up at 4:30 the next morning to get ready for work, the whole dream seemed crazy. I couldn't marry her anyway. There was a $6,000 debt hanging over my head. Even if there weren't, I couldn't spend a lifetime on the plantation. It was only a crude dream a caveman might have. You were in your warm secure cave with enough food and your own woman while a storm and wild beasts raged outside. The shadows and shapes which seemed so solid at night evaporated in the daylight. You couldn't blot out the rest of the world during the day, it was everywhere, oppressive, top-heavy, leaning on you. I thought of going to the drugstore in Pepelau to get some rubbers. Sachan would let me. But if I didn't marry her, that would be worse than doing it with a pig. At least you didn't give the pig false hopes or ruin its reputation.

It rained so continually a damp smell of the outhouse hung over Pig Pen Avenue. The camp, I realized then, was planned and built around its sewage system. The half dozen rows of underground concrete ditches, two feet wide and three feet deep, ran from the higher slope of camp into the concrete irrigation ditch on the lower perimeter of camp. An outhouse built over the sewage ditch had two pairs of back-to-back toilets and serviced four houses. Shit too was organized according to the plantation pyramid. Mr. Nelson was top shit on the highest slope, then there were the Portuguese, Spanish, and *nisei lunas* with their indoor toilets which flushed into the same ditches, then Japanese Camp, and Filipino Camp.

Everything was over-organized. There were sports to keep you busy and happy in your spare time. Even the churches seemed part of the scheme to keep you contented. Mr. Nelson knew each of us by first name, knew each family, and asked each time anxiously about the family. He acted like a father, and he looked after you and cared for you provided you didn't disobey. Union talk was disobedience and treason, and if you were caught talking it or organizing, you were fired and your family and your belongings dumped on the "government" road.

I kept wishing Snooky had come back to teach at Kahana. I'd go to talk to him. He was the only guy who helped you to see things as they were out there. The others ignored your questions or what they saw out there, or tried to make you see only the things they wanted you to see. He talked of freedom, while everybody else talked of duty and obligation. It was like we were born in a cage and Snooky was coaxing us to fly off, not run away, but be on our own and taste the freedom and danger of the open space. Rumor was that he had gone to Spain to fight in the Civil War back in 1937.

Snooky gave me a glimpse of what it could be. I would have to get out and be on my own even if the old man was successful and he was doing me the favors, even if the plantation made me its highest *luna*. Freedom was freedom from other people's shit, and shit was shit no matter how lovingly it was dished, how high or low it came from. Shit was the glue which held a group together, and I was going to have no part of any shit or any group.

22

In January 1943 the Army asked for 1,500 *nisei* volunteers. We would form an all-*nisei* regiment with volunteers from the mainland and be allowed to fight in Europe. There were already six Kahana boys among the over one thousand *niseis* in the 100th Infantry Battalion training in the states for combat in Europe.

"You shouldn't volunteer," mother said at the supper table. "Toshio has been of little help as number one son, and we're depending on you to help the family. You understand?"

"Every family should send at least one son," I said.

"But you're our only son now. We're poor and poor families have to be more careful. Acting as an individual is a luxury only the rich can afford. The poorer you are the more you have to be united. Acting on your own when you're so poor is selfishness. We're not only poor, our number one son hasn't been of much help. Families with good number one sons have been able to send the younger children to college. Being so poor, we have to be excused, we have to think of the family first . . ."

I couldn't blow up like Tosh, but I'd learned not to jump at her bait. Once upon a time I'd have said yes, just to reassure her and shut her up. But Tosh kept saying, "No go fall for her sob story. She goin' hold you to your *samurai's* word."

"You goin' join?" Tsuneko said in pidgin.

"I doan know."

The next day I had "Crisco" stop by at the Courthouse in Pepelau when we went to the mill, and I signed up. "I wish I can go too," "Crisco" said, "I wanna get out of here. I sick of this life, but my kid brother going, and I better stay and help the family."

When I got home from work that day I said, "I volunteered."

Tears rolled down mother's cheeks. "Why don't you listen to what I say?"

I shrugged. "It can't be helped."

"What will happen to our debt?"

"If I die, there's $10,000 insurance you will get. If I live, I'll come back and help you."

"What if you get hurt and become a cripple?"

"It can't be helped. I'll make $50 a month in the Army, same as I'm getting. I'll send you $40 a month."

"I kept thinking when Jyun was born Why? Why? Is he to be your substitute?"

"Don't be silly."

The next day mother started sewing my *sennin bari.* It was like one of her rush orders. She sewed the first stitch on the crimson silk sash, then rushed to each house in camp to ask the women to sew in a stitch. This thousand-stitch sash was supposed to be a good luck charm. It was what she remembered doing for the soldiers leaving for the Russo-Japanese War in 1904. The other mothers with volunteer sons were doing the same thing.

Mr. Kuni and the older *niseis* went to talk to the ones who hadn't volunteered, "I'd go if I were young. I'd jump at this chance to see Europe. It's a free trip." That wasn't the point. Everybody in Kahana was dying to get out of this icky shit-hole, and here was his chance delivered on a silver platter. Besides, once you fought, you earned the right to complain and participate, you earned a right to a future.

In a couple of weeks nearly everybody single and healthy in Kahana volunteered and there would be a plantation truck the next day to take us to the plantation hospital for a physical. They chose twelve of us out of fifty. Every family went to say goodbye to the twelve families, bringing *sembetsu* (a parting gift of money in a white letter envelope). Mother kept a record of each gift, ranging from $2 to $20, and she gave the other eleven families the same amount they'd given me. I got $300 in all, and gave half of it to mother. Then there was a big party for the twelve of us, and the next day we left for Pepelau to join the volunteers from there. Mother had me eat an orange and leave from the front door.

23

It was my first time away from home. It was the first time I had over $25 in my pocket. There was the continual hubbub of over 2,500 guys packed into a small space, of whom I knew only about thirty from the Kahana-Pepelau area. Every time there was a pause from all the waiting and standing in line, crap games sprang up in the barracks and on the red dirt. Everybody had money and every third guy was a crapshooter. The sight of all that money drove me mad. There was $25,000 at least floating around in the crap games. A few played poker, but that was too slow. The mass of players and spectators bunched around the crap games. Most of the games were played on blankets on barrack floors, the dice rolled by hand. There were a few guys who rolled the dice the way Hiroshi did at the Citizens' Quarters in Kahana. The dice didn't bounce but rolled out in unison like the wheels of a cart. There had to be an advantage to that. Hiroshi never lost.

I bought a pair of dice and got a paper and pencil, and examined the dice. The opposite sides of a cube always totaled 7. There were thirty-six combinations of numbers, starting with 12 (6 and 6), which happened once. 6 and 5 happened twice; a 10 happened three ways, 5 and 5, 6 and 4, 4 and 6, and so forth. There were four ways of making 9; five ways of making 8; and six ways of making 7. So the odds against 10 was 3 to 6; against 9 was 4 to 6; against 8 was 5 to 6. And 4, 9, 8, were mates of 10, 5, 6 respectively and took the same odds. But there had to be some magic in combining certain numbers so they'd form the axis of the roll, and not show up as one of the numbers. They'd be dead numbers. After several tries, I came up with the combination:

1st die	2nd die	
1	1	If I used 1 and 6 as the axis, there'd be no
2	2	2's, 3's or 12's, or no craps on the first
3	3	throw. This would be the combination on
4	4	the initial roll.
5	5	
6	6	
1	1	If I buried the 1/6 on the first die and 2/5
2	2	on the second, 7 would happen two ways
3	3	4-3 and 3-4, and 6 or 8 would happen three
4	4	ways. Odds would be 3 to 2 in my favor
5	5	of 5 to 6.
6	6	

1̸	1	This final combination made the odds for
2	2	10, 4, 9, 5, at 2 to 2, instead of the regular
3	3̸	2 to 1 for 4 and 10, and 3 to 2 for 9 and 5.
4	4̸	
5	5	
6̸	6	

It floored me. You eliminated all chance of crapping out in the first roll. Your chance of making 6-8 was 3 to 2 in your favor; 9-5 or 10-4 was 50-50! And it wasn't really cheating. The others had the option of stopping any of your rolls, or they could play with a cup, or have the roller bang the dice against the wall, or use a canvas or the bare floor instead of a blanket. The next question was whether I could do it. I had long fingers and I could pick up the dice quickly in whatever combination. I practiced on my bunk, and after a couple of hours I felt I was ready. I had $150 in my pocket, I'd never gambled before.

The first time I picked up the dice I shook all over, my fingers were thick *chorizos,* the dice barely rattled when I shook them, and the roll bounced and one die flipped on its side. I rolled again and they bounced all over the place without crapping. My third roll improved 100 percent. By the fifth time I was still shaking inside, but the dice were rolling out of my palm like the smooth unfolding of a carpet.

I made $300 the first day, and I couldn't sleep that night, I couldn't slow down, there was a fire in my brain, all I could think of was $6,000 and all the money everywhere. I'd been chicken today, I had to force myself to believe in those odds all the way. $6,000 or bust. There were several who rolled that way, and whenever they came into the game when I was rolling, they bet with me.

"Where you learn to padroll?" one of them asked me.

"What?"

"Who taught you to padroll?"

"I learned by watching you."

"No play, you."

The next day the games you could padroll in were fewer. More and more people were playing with cups. I had to do it quick. Every time we had a break I went stalking for a game. I stood in long lines waiting for injections, waiting for shoes, waiting for a break. I was living on my nerves, without a wink of sleep, I could think of only six g's. It was out there waiting for me.

I'd thrown six passes the day before but I'd pulled it in after three passes. And I'd bet $10 and $20 to start with. Now I layed down $100 for the first roll. 200, 400, 800, 1,600, 3,200, 6,400. I needed six passes. After the third pass I had to force myself, and my voice came out choked, "Shoot it." At 1,600 my hands were shaking. Maybe it's only in my head. But I had to go through with it. I had to believe in the odds I had worked out on paper. No chance of crapping out in the first roll. Four out of sixteen chances of throwing a natural. "Shoot it," I left most of my voice back in my throat. The guys peeled off 10's and 20's till they covered 1,600. I threw a 10. I still had a 50-50 chance of making 10. After several more throws, a 7 came up.

I walked off crushed. I let $1,600 get away. I should've dragged. But another part of me said, no, you did right. Believe in the odds. That's the only way. No time for playing chicken. I had one whole day of testing.

After supper that night we had to stand in more lines. It was nine before I was free, and I went looking for the biggest padroll game. I edged myself into the circle of players and faded 5's and 10's, and waited my turn at the dice. "Shoot 200," I got down on one knee and picked up the dice. "Give me some room" I swung my right arm in an arc, making enough room for a good back swing. 400, 800, 1,600, 3,200, 6,400. I needed five passes for my magic six g's. Go for broke. Have absolute faith in the odds. I wasn't fighting myself anymore. "Shoot it," I said each time I made my point, my voice no longer stuck in my throat. I felt numb, all skin and senses flushed and coated with a thin film, slowing down my reflexes. All the money on the blanket didn't seem like real money you bought groceries with. I threw my fourth pass. One more to go! "Shoot it," I said, and looked at the circle of faces. Thank God, they were all strangers.

Somebody covered 20, then 20 more, 100, 150, till 1,000 was covered. "Here's two g's," somebody dropped a wad of money onto the blanket. He stood on the outside, had been just standing and watching till now, mid-thirtyish, curly black hair, stocky, heavy biceps of a wrestler. I quickly counted his 2,000 and matched it with 2,000 from the pot. "Any more?" "You too hot," somebody said.

I held the uncovered 200 in my left hand and picked up the dice, burying 6 and 1, and rattled them against each other, not disturbing the 6-1 axis, and swung back and rolled them out on the blanket in a smooth follow-through.

"Wait a minute," the big fader dived over a kneeling player and grabbed the rolling dice before they came to a stop.

He stood up, "How about using a cup? Anybody got a cup?"

"Okay," he edged himself into the inner circle, "how about banging it against the wall then? Make some room there," he cleared the area next to the wall.

I was suddenly back in my own skin, the numbness had peeled off, but I felt calm. If my luck was so bad I couldn't throw one pass on the up-and-up, then I deserved to lose, it was my proper *bachi.* I remembered the joke about the guy who was so hard luck, he jumped over the *pali* to commit suicide and got blown back up by the wind. I too am cursed with the Oyama luck if I can't throw one honest pass. Nothing I do will help, I can only lay low and not take any chances and wait for the bad luck to pass.

"Okay?" the big fader kneeled next to me. Even heavy features unsmiling.

I threw down the 200 in my left hand. "Here's 200 more. All or nothing."

He dug into his front pockets and then his back pocket and uncrumpled 5's and 10's and 20's and counted out 200.

I grabbed the dice and shook them every which way, "Here we go, baby, give me a natural!" and slammed them against the wall like they were a softball I was pitching. They flew back like a pair of frightened grasshoppers, and for a split second I saw two 6's, my heart dropped like a lead lump into my stomach, then one flipped over almost in slow motion, and showed a 5!

I felt like busting out into a song and dance! I've been freed! I've made my bail money out of this prison of filial piety and family unity! Out of ten more miserable years on the plantation! I took a deep breath and tried to keep my hands from shaking as I scooped in the pile of money, and arranged it in separate piles of 50's, 20's, 10's, 5's. Then I counted out 1,000 and put it in the center of the blanket. "Shoot it," I said weakly. I had to give them a chance to make back some of it. When nobody moved, I took out 500, "Shoot that then!"

"You been bust me," the heavy bettor said.

"Yeah, you been bust up the game," somebody said.

I picked up the 500, "Whose dice?"

"Mine."

I peeled off 200 and gave it to him, then I counted another 200 and gave it to the heavy bettor. Then I stuffed the rest of the money into all six pockets of my fatigues, and walked out. Once outside I was hopscotching and skip-jumping like a kid with an awkward hard-on.

"Hey, Lucky! Hey, Kyo!" Bob Kaita, a real talkative kid, came running after me in the dark.

"What?" I slowed down. He was about five feet tall and looked fifteen, and he'd gotten to know nearly everybody in a few days.

"You know what I been hear?"

"What?"

He strode beside me, "I been hear you never been gamble before. The guys from your hometown been tell me. Yeah. They tell me you never been gamble before. No gamble, no drink, no play with girls, real quiet type."

"That's right."

"Caw-mon!"

"That's a fact."

"Boy, your hometown must grow bullshit."

I couldn't sleep all night, $6,130 bulging in my pockets. I'd sleep and wake up and find out it was a dream. It'd been too easy. Like my left hook was so good I got to be another Henry Armstrong without all that roadwork. And it wasn't really cheating, not like marked cards or loaded dice anyway. Besides, if I didn't take their money, another padroller would've. It was their fault if they couldn't spot it. In gambling it was dog eat dog, every dog was after something for nothing, you never gave a dog an even break.

But no matter how many excuses I came up with, I felt bad. I had jumped in with two feet, without hesitation, nervous only that I might not execute right. I'd jumped in with eyes wide open, knowing it was crooked. How far would I have gone? I wouldn't have used loaded or crooked dice. I wouldn't have kept on padrolling after six g's. What if the debt had been ten g's? Twenty? At least $3,200 was honest in spite of myself, and I didn't feel bad enough to return the other 3,200.

The next day I went to a bank in Wahiawa, a few miles from Schofield, and sent Tosh a check for $6,000 and scribbled a note: "Won this in crap game. Pay up all the debt. I manufactured some of the luck, but I think the Oyama luck has finally turned around. Take care the body. See you after the War."

THE END

Afterword

THE HAWAII NISEI:
TOUGH TALK AND SWEET SUGAR

Franklin S. Odo

The most important feature of Milton Murayama's brilliant *All I Asking for Is My Body* is the quality of the storytelling. It deserves thorough discussion and criticism among literary professionals and students. The work has a further genius, however, in its evocation of several major topics in modern Hawaiian history, specifically during the 1930s, the decade before United States involvement in World War II. In this brief Afterword, I suggest that Murayama's novel provides us with valuable insights into the worlds of language, sugar plantation history, and the second-generation Japanese Americans, the *nisei*.

Murayama gives us an almost tangible feel for the language—pidgin English or, more correctly, Hawaiian English Creole—then in use among the *nisei* on a Maui sugar plantation. The details are important because the forms or dialects of pidgin differed among groups and over time. Second, he gives us a vivid picture of these workers' lives on a sugar plantation: those crucibles in which so much of modern Hawaii would be formed. Finally, he knows that these *nisei* children of the Japanese immigrants were already a potent force in the social, economic, and political spheres of Island life and he breathes much needed life into their story. All of these topics remain extraordinarily significant on both intellectual and practical levels.

Murayama intended to reach the broadest possible audience with this book and thus limited his use of pidgin, confining it to conversation and, even there, tempering the language to make it accessible to standard English speakers. In a literary conference held in 1980, Murayama recalled: "When I was writing 'I'll Crack Your Head Kotsun' I was thinking of the *New Yorker, Harper,* and the *Atlantic.* I wanted my pidgin to be understood by the editors and readers of those magazines. I don't remember stopping to analyze how I was going to do this, but . . . what I did was three things: use phonetic spelling only on a few words which didn't occur too often, use the syntax and rhythms of pidgin in the dialogue, and use standard English in the narration except for a few pidgin expressions."[1]

Critic Rob Wilson noted: "Part of the accomplishment of the novel is that the language ranges from the vernacular to the literate and standard, and so reflects the cultural and linguistic diversity of Hawaii."[2] In the novel, Murayama uses standard English and pidgin. In real life, the narrator Kiyo explains, "we spoke four languages: good English in school, pidgin English among ourselves, good or pidgin Japanese to our parents and the other old folks" (p.5). The wonder is that Murayama emerged using any one of the languages well. For most, that experience proved to be an insuperable barrier to good creative writing. It is difficult, in fact, to find other *nisei* writers of the same quality. Murayama himself provides one important clue to understanding the relative lack of literary output from this group; "good" English was standard English; pidgin was bad and had to be eliminated or, at best, tolerated outside the classroom. In the process, pidgin-speakers learned that their language and culture were inferior. As a direct result, youngsters like Michie, in the novel, who make determined efforts to avoid the use of pidgin are "identifying with the ruling and outside class, even [committing] an act of racial betrayal."[3] These are, unhappily, continuing policy issues despite the overwhelming evidence that Hawaiian Creole English is a legitimate language with an integrity of its own; that the language deserves respect; that its speakers will continue to use it, often at their own educational and employment risk; and that there are established pedagogies to allow for the encouragement of both languages, in school and out.[4]

Arnold Hiura, editor of the fine publication, *The Hawaii Herald,* considers *All I Asking for Is My Body* to be the "only comprehensive literary treatment of the Hawaii plantation experience, an experience which either directly or indirectly affects a very large segment of Hawaii's population."[5] Of course, Murayama does not pretend to write about the lives of the plantation managers; he does not even attempt to penetrate the upper levels of the plantation work force such as the *luna,* or overseers; and he does not contrive stories about the other ethnic communities on the plantation—the Filipinos or Portuguese or Koreans or, even, the Okinawans. But these end up as strengths in this work because the texture and details of this Oyama family provide insights into other groups and invite us to imagine their lives and, perhaps, encourage more creative pieces from writers who are as observant and skilled as Murayama is. There are, to be sure, recent histories, including those by Edward Beechert and Ronald Takaki, which help illuminate the lives of sugar workers.[6] And the collections and exhibitions of institutions like the Waipahu

Cultural Garden Park, Alexander and Baldwin Sugar Museum, and the Bishop Museum do much to help us recall that period. But the fact remains that Hiura is all too accurate. We do not have much more in the way of creative literature about the industrial way of life that dominated the years between the mid-nineteenth and mid-twentieth centuries nor about the lives of hundreds of thousands of native Hawaiians and immigrant families.

Murayama allows us to feel the degree of isolation in the more remote plantation camps and the importance of something like boxing for the *nisei* who wanted to get out. He provides the sights and smells (for those who can remember) of the whole camp which he "realized then, was planned and built around its sewage system. The half dozen rows of underground concrete ditches, two feet wide and three feet deep, ran from the higher slope of camp into the concrete irrigation ditch on the lower perimeter of camp. . . . Shit too was organized according to the plantation pyramid. Mr. Nelson [camp overseer] was top shit on the highest slope, then there were the Portuguese, Spanish, and *nisei luna*s with their indoor toilets which flushed into the same ditches, then Japanese Camp, and Filipino Camp" (p. 96).

But, in a fascinating section, Murayama introduces us to a strike on the plantation and the eighth grade teacher, Mr. Snook, who is a recent arrival to the Islands. "Snooky" is appalled at the willingness of his students to accept the status quo, especially the fact that "the plantation divides and rules, and you the exploited are perfectly happy to be divided and ruled. . . . The Filipinos strike, and you are all too happy to break that strike." In fact, Murayama uses some actual history and cites Ray Stannard Baker who called Hawaii's plantation system "the last surviving vestige of feudalism in the United States" (p. 33). Snook, of course, is not back the next year. Kiyo tells his older brother Tosh about Snook and the latter responds: "He a Communist or a queer. Nice *haoles* always after something else" (p. 36).

While now dwarfed by tourism and military spending, sugar continues to be critically important to the economy. Lucy Jokiel, in an article in the October 1987 issue of *Hawaii Business,* wondered whether management arrogance and "condescending" attitudes toward workers, leftovers from the sugar plantation past, contribute to Hawaii's abysmally low wages.[7]

The year 1985 marked the centennial of the arrival of government contract laborers from Japan to work in Hawaii's sugar plantations. A wide variety of publications emerged to describe that century of life for the immigrants and their descendants.[8] Notably missing, however, was any significant reference to or publication of creative writing from the Japanese American community.

All I Asking for Is My Body is the most compelling work done on the Hawaii *nisei* experience. Murayama understood his theme to be "the Japanese family system vs. individualism, the plantation system vs. individualism. And so the environments of the family and the plantation are inseparable from the theme."[9] Fortunately for us as readers, however, he understood that the story was the key ingredient; that anything less would simply add to the sociological study of the plantation and the Japanese family in Hawaii. Hiura put it more powerfully: "In the case of Hawaii's Japanese Americans, it almost seems as if this rule of saving family face has been extrapolated out to include our entire ethnic group. . . . we have, in fact, just histories and sociological studies on the plantation, but almost none that deal with it on a literary level. . . . we have been denied, up to this work, an idea of what the real, human situation of the plantation has been. . . . we've come up with a kind of generalized myth of what the Japanese American experience has been."[10]

In this work, Murayama explodes another myth, that of the melting pot, by describing how separate were the lives of the various ethnic communities in spite of the physical and social environments. The Oyama family members, even the younger *nisei,* do not have any real access to other groups; the Portuguese, Spanish, Filipinos all exist as foils for the Japanese unit. This observation is surely no grounds for criticism. Murayama writes what he knows, and he acknowledges: "there was a hierarchy and a separation of races, which was done deliberately by the plantation so that there wouldn't be any cohesion among labor. But even then, there was an intrinsic sort of snobbery within each group (whose children) didn't play with the other groups. . . . the only time I have any account of another race is the work gang situation where Kiyo is working with the Filipino gang. Even then, he doesn't know what the insides of their houses look like or what they do after they go home."[11] Kiyo does know the insides of one home in the Filipino Camp—that of Makot's mother who is the resident prostitute for the Filipino laborers. This point is important because it is dramatic evidence of the limitations of the concept of "localism" for either analysis or social action.

Murayama details the way in which traditional religious observances are passed through the generations and the vehemence with which powerful values like filial piety are resisted and defied. He even takes us, all too briefly, into the controversial world of the

Japanese language newspapers when Tosh argues with his father the relative merits of the editors of the two leading dailies. One counsels moderation and conciliation toward the planters during the Filipino strike; the other urges militant support of the Filipinos and a strategy of Americanization that involved both cutting ties to Japan and fighting for civil and human rights in the United States.[12] In a scene reminiscent of the one described in Daniel Inouye's *Journey to Washington*,[13] Tosh is punished for misbehavior in Japanese language class, runs away from school and refuses to go back even after his father humbly apologizes for the son's actions (p. 49).

The watershed years for the *nisei* are those of World War II. For them, the question was not one of identity; they were overwhelmingly convinced of their ethnic background and their national loyalties. As the oldest son, Tosh takes over by ordering his father, after learning of the Pearl Harbor attack: "You have a Japanese flag in the *tansu* [dresser]. Burn it or bury it. Hide all your Japanese books in the chicken coop. Don't talk in Japanese when there're any non-Japanese around" (p. 78).

Kiyo is different. He wonders about the war and about the full range of traditional values the Japanese were assumed to cherish. The sneak attack on Pearl Harbor devastated many *nisei*. Kiyo, at least, had an unusual teacher, Mr. Takemoto, who could discuss these and all difficult issues. Even at the end of a long and fascinating conversation dealing with a range of issues plaguing him, however, Kiyo is left with a sensibility Mr. Takemoto could not be expected to appreciate: "The once proud ground I'd been standing on had turned into soft shit, and I became a zombie. I'd stare at mother and father for long periods, I'd walk and walk in the night. I felt a flutter of pride when they sank the *Prince of Wales* and *Repulse*. At least they can fight without a sneak attack. But it wasn't a racial war, they were like a disease, and the sooner they were beaten the better. It was like watching your older brother whom you'd believed in and loved now running wild committing murders" (p. 83).

Milton Murayama's work has recreated and reinterpreted a world that no longer exists. But, as he suggested at the 1980 conference, "I feel nostalgic about the plantation camp, but I *don't* grieve its passing." Hiura, too, warned about falling into the trap of excessive romanticizing of the plantation past: "you try living in a house like that: the toilet is outside, there's wind coming in between the boards, there's splinters. It may seem kind of pretty from afar, but it's not fun to live in." And, in the end, Murayama summed it up with his sense of who had/has control by insisting that "the whole question is not in our hands. It's in the hands of Amfac or whoever owns the plantation, whether it's making money, enough money to be worth all of their efforts.''[14]

Notes

1. Eric Chock and Jody Manabe, eds., *Writers of Hawaii: A Focus on Our Literary Heritage* (Honolulu, Bamboo Ridge Press, 1981) 61.

2. Ibid., 63.

3. Ibid., 64.

4. For the most recent of a long line of treatments extending back to the pioneer in this field, John Reinecke, see Glenn Gilbert, ed., *Pidgin and Creole Languages: Essays in Memory of John E. Reinecke* (Honolulu, University of Hawaii Press, 1987).

5. Chock and Manabe, *Writers,* 65.

6. Edward D. Beechert, *Working in Hawaii: A Labor History* (Honolulu, University of Hawaii Press, 1985; Ronald Takaki, *Pau Hana: Plantation Life and Labor in Hawaii* (Honolulu, University of Hawaii Press, 1983).

7. Lucy Jokiel, ''Plantation Mentality,'' *Hawaii Business* (October 1987):27–28.

8. See, for example, Roland Kotani, *The Japanese in Hawaii: A Century of Struggle* (Honolulu: Hawaii Hochi, 1985); Franklin Odo and Kazuko Sinoto, *A Pictorial History of the Japanese in Hawaii, 1885–1924* (Honolulu: Bishop Museum Press, 1985); Dorothy Hazama and Jane Komeiji, *Okagesamade: The Japanese in Hawaii* (Honolulu: Bess Press, 1986).

9. Chock and Manabe, *Writers,* 60.

10. Ibid., 66.

11. Ibid., 68–69.

12. Real-life models were Yasutaro Soga of the *Nippu Jiji* and Kinzaburo Makino of the *Hawaii Hochi.* See Yasutaro (Keiho) Soga, *Gojunenkan no Hawaii kaiko* [Recollections of fifty years in Hawaii] (Honolulu: Gojunenkan Association, 1953); and Makino Biography Committee, *Life of Kinzaburo Makino* (Honolulu: Michie Makino, 1965).

13. Daniel Inouye, *Journey to Washington* (Englewood Cliffs, N.J.: Prentice-Hall, 1967).

14. Chock and Manabe, *Writers,* 69.

About the Author

Milton Atsushi Murayama was born in Lahaina, Maui, and grew up in Lahaina and on "Pig Pen Avenue" in Puukolii. The plantation camp, once home to over six hundred, no longer exists. He attended Lahainaluna High School. During World War II he trained at the Military Intelligence Language School at Camp Savage, Minnesota, and served as an interpreter in India and China. Murayama received a B.A. in English from the University of Hawaii, and an M.A. in Chinese and Japanese from Columbia University. He has lived in Minneapolis, New York, and Washington, D.C., and presently resides in San Francisco with his wife. Among his works are three plays, one of them based on *All I Asking for Is My Body*. He is currently writing a longer novel about the Oyama family.